WOLF MEAT

Link Sawle was determined to seek revenge on his father's killer and, with his friend Bose Marshfield, he trails hundreds of miles to Colorado Springs. There he soon becomes entangled with double-dealings, family feuds, cattle rustling and even murder. Then there is the psychotic outlaw, Dog Kerlue, to be faced. Surprise follows surprise when Link finds out about his mother's disappearance and learns shattering news about a notorious outlaw called Boy Wales. Suddenly Link's world is turned upside down.

Books by Caleb Rand
in the Linford Western Library:

THE EVIL STAR

CALEB RAND

WOLF MEAT

Complete and Unabridged

LINFORD
Leicester

First published in Great Britain in 2002 by
Robert Hale Limited
London

First Linford Edition
published 2003
by arrangement with
Robert Hale Limited
London

British Library CIP Data

Rand, Caleb
  Wolf meat.—Large print ed.—
Linford western library
1. Western stories
2. Large type books
I. Title
813.5'4 [F]

ISBN 0–7089–9484–9

Published by
F. A. Thorpe (Publishing)
Anstey, Leicestershire

Set by Words & Graphics Ltd.
Anstey, Leicestershire
Printed and bound in Great Britain by
T. J. International Ltd., Padstow, Cornwall

This book is printed on acid-free paper

1

The Chase

Leaves were tawny, edged with frost in the arroyos, and streamers of snow lay white along the jagged mane of the Sangre de Cristos. There were hard, stubborn qualities to the land, and it reflected in the small herd of wild horses that grazed below the timberline.

An hour had passed and the grulla stallion was still visible. Young Jackson Sawle had collected his thoughts, made up his mind to go into the foot chase.

Conserving his strength, he went off at a steady lope: the long-distance endurance run. He cut between the stallion and the mares, giving the big horse something new to worry about.

After two unremitting hours, the stallion appeared to be tiring of its line, but it never slackened. They'd run away from the setting sun, and when the last darkness finally came, the stallion was still resolute in its flight.

Jack had his blanket tied in a roll across his back. He found a shallow scrape, and curled on his side, his body outline just below the flat of the land.

The night layered down cold, and at first light, Jack stood and shook the frosty cut from his blanket. He looked out towards the stallion, smiled grimly, and started into another run. They were still separated by a good mile, but twice during the morning he closed to within hundreds of yards.

Jack knew the time was approaching when he could make a move. He kneeled, looked east into the pale rising sun, and squeezed hard on the rawhide bolas.

The stallion was now slightly less than a hundred yards ahead of Jack. It was fronting him, still alert, but looking wearied. Jack knew that the wild strength would return at the first sign of danger. The grulla would fight like a demon in the face of capture.

The wintry sun was back-lighting the stallion, and Jack couldn't take his eyes away. He hardly dared blink, for fear the horse would be gone. He watched anxiously as it broke into a faltering trot through the packed mud that bordered the creek. Jack had his flask, but he knew the horse wouldn't go much further without a drink.

He took time, and worked himself downwind. He eased closer, taking cover advantage of tumbleweed and gnarled willow. From across the creek, the stallion was nervous, and made slight cries of anguish as it lowered its nose into the chilly water.

From forty feet, Jack knew it was the closest he would get. He raised himself, took one long backswing, and hurled the bolas low across the surface of the creek. He saw the whirling strips coil into the stallion, the hide pellets squeezing low around its big forelegs.

He scythed his way fast through the shallow creek, straight at the falling

3

horse. It was already thrashing in an attempt to disentangle itself from the cut of the bolas. Jack threw himself onto the big wild head. He forced the stallion's ears to the ground, locking the fingers of his right hand under the horse's jaw. He drew the great grey muzzle towards him, pulling and twisting the gleaming neck into his body. The stallion continued to struggle and lash out with his hind feet, and Jack felt a wild blast from its nostrils scorching the side of his face. He hung on, bracing every muscle against the pull of the grulla.

They lay in the desert sand for an hour and, as Jack felt an ebb of the stallion's struggle, his hands and leg muscles relaxed a little. It was a crucial moment, and he cautiously began to free one of his hands. He untied his bandanna and laid it across the big fearful eyes, then unwound a knotted cord from around his waist. He worked it under and over the stallion's head, tentative and easy, taking care not to release too much pressure. He made the cord into a slip-noose, and worked it through the long, thick mane.

When the stallion climbed to its feet, there'd be trouble, and Jack would be in a vulnerable position. A strike from any hoof would be lethal. He set himself hard against the renewed pulling of the horse's head. If it got its nose and powerful neck free, Jack would be joining the big 'skeeters' that clouded the banks of the creek.

Jack's shoulders and arms were beginning to spasm with strain. Every time he loosened his hold, even a little, the stallion sensed it and immediately renewed its pressure. It would be a long and debilitating contest. Jack didn't know whether he could hold out or not, and once again, first dark was approaching. He was hungry now, his water was finished and he felt numbness creeping through him.

He felt a tremble through the stallion's neck, and he instinctively released his hold. The stallion rolled, snorted wildly and surged upward. The bolas had loosened, and it dropped away from the stallion's front feet. The lunge almost lifted Jack clear of the ground, and he clung on in desperation. The stallion leaped forward in a frantic bucking run, shaking his head and squealing, swinging wide against Jack's sweat-soaked arms. The rope was hanging free, and they were off running. Jack was dragged, the toes of his skin boots stabbing furrows across the flats.

After several hundred yards, the stallion knew it wasn't gaining freedom. It powered into a sudden check, swinging Jack ahead of its stand. Jack's heart was pounding with elation or terror, he didn't know which. He fought to gain his footing. He was breathless, but managed to wheeze incantations into the tiring stallion's ear. His voice was cracked and shook with emotion.

The tension was flowing away, and Jack took hold of the rope, just below the stallion's great jowls. Then he let his fingers slip, slow but deliberate, until he had a six-foot lead. He tugged gently on the rope, and laughed in amazement. By the open movement, he'd offered the stallion its freedom.

Jack let the end of the rope trail away. He walked exhausted back to the creek, staring at the ground ahead of him. He saw the wavering shadow move alongside, then the stallion's nose nudged him between his sagging shoulder blades. In letting the horse have a choice, he'd made the first smart move of what he hoped was a lasting alliance.

2

Bad Night

Bose Marshfield sat with Lincoln Sawle. The grizzled wrinkle-horn had ridden out to intercept Link on his return to the ranch. For the third, fourth time, Bose had given him what few details there were to tell.

'I guess we won't ever know what really happened.'

'I *will* find out what happened,' Link pronounced. 'You say they left his body for the buzzards . . . the dogs?'

'Yeah, I'm sorry, Link, that's what it looked like. They had stolen cattle with 'em . . . weren't about to give him a burial service.'

'They murdered him . . . a man who'd never carried a gun. I'll be goin' after 'em in the mornin',' Link threatened, as he crawled under his blanket and slicker.

But there was no sleep. Link couldn't understand why he was so stirred up about losing a father he'd never really held any affection for. Link had been no more than knee-high, when his mother had run from the ranch, gone back to her family in Pueblo. Worse, she'd taken Link's brother, Jackson, with her.

For the next ten years, Link spent very little time at home with his father. Bose had found him a little rimrock filly, and when Elias Sawle went on his small-time cattle deals to Tucumcari or Santa Rosa, Link was off fishing for catfish that roamed the seep-water pools of the Punta de Agua.

But everything had moved on, changed now, and Sawle history didn't bring him any comfort. It was an hour before dawn when he saddled his horse, turned to face Bose.

'Maybe for once I should've let them fish be . . . left them goddamn kids rods at home,' he said broodingly.

Bose was ready with his reply. 'Yeah. I figured you'd think that. But the taste

9

of them bullheads linger, an' I'd say you were wrong. Anyways, there ain't much you could o' done about it. Your pa was never goin' to take you with him to sell a cow or two.' Bose knew there wasn't much Link knew about his own father. He cursed as he stretched his back, grimaced at the bone-aches of cold rising. 'An' you'll be needin' me to show you where I buried him,' he said. 'The Plain's a mighty difficult place to find anythin'.'

Link nodded and that was that. The two men rode east, into the sunrise, to look for Elias Sawle's killers.

★ ★ ★

A *blue whistler* was sweeping across the bleak, waterless stretch of desolation known as the Staked Plain. It was late Fall and the raw wind bit into the marrow of a man's bones. Link's face was grey-blue with cold and his legs felt numb. Bose must have suffered more than he did, for his blood was thinner, but neither of them complained.

Bose guided them across a hundred-mile strip of New Mexico. He rode south, bent their trail to the west a little, where they could strike water at Beck's Landing on the Pecos. Link reckoned it was something other than sentiment that made Bose head them into the daggers of a blizzard to look for a desert grave.

It was approaching first dark and the dry snow stung their eyes, made their face muscles ache with tension. Bose halted them beside the carcasses of what had been two covered freight wagons. Charred wooden ribs showed through snow that covered soil too arid even to grow creosote. 'What do you make of this?' he asked, as their horses swung their rumps to the *whistler*.

Link looked around for burial signs, but saw nothing. 'Injuns?' he suggested.

'No, Link. I'd o' known if they'd been killed by Apache. I told you, I buried most of 'em . . . most of what the coyote had left. I found your pa about five miles from here . . . followed the tracks of his mule. He'd been with these wagons all right. Whoever did *this*, trailed him. He saw what they'd done, an' that's why he died, Link.'

'We were never more'n a siwash outfit, Bose. What was he doin' with that lot?'

'Don't know, son. Perhaps he just ran into 'em. But you're right . . . nobody had reason to *kill* him . . . not that I know of.'

'Who the hell do you reckon these men were then?'

'I *know* who they were, Link. A Pool herd from Texas. They were makin' for the Goodnight-Lovin' trail . . . headed for Cimarron. They were a tough crew, an' probably some of 'em weren't much better than the scum who shot 'em up.'

'How do you know this, Bose?' Link interrupted.

'I met 'em out on the Brazos. They weren't too friendly, and I only stayed one night. There was ten of 'em in the outfit.'

12

'What's so important about that?'

'I buried what was left of six of 'em.'

Link had a few seconds of thought. 'Right,' he said. 'That means four got away.'

'Well, they didn't get killed here.' Bose sat with his arms pulled in close to his chest. 'Maybe they were trailed . . . shot down like Elias,' he reflected. 'Maybe they threw in together after the shootin'. Maybe one or two of 'em was already in tow. Maybe they're alive . . . headed north.'

'Yeah, maybe,' Link said acidly, as he edged his mare in a tight circle, steadied it against the piercing wind. 'You'll know 'em, Bose . . . them four you didn't get to plant out,' he suggested.

'Yeah, I'll know 'em, son.'

That night, their water was running low, and after marking his father's grave with the blackened remains of a tailgate, Link couldn't bring himself to burn wood for a camp-fire. He tended to the horses while Bose flamed up a

13

pile of cow chips to cook strong coffee and meat pieces. The night seemed all the colder for the lack of a good fire and the snow stung like frozen sand.

To escape the bleakness and chilling wind they crawled under their blankets with their meagre grub. After they'd eaten, Bose talked through the night and Link listened quietly to the man's thoughts.

'These men you'll want to be goin' after, son, remember only one of 'em shot him. You can't track, an' kill 'em all. Elias wouldn't o' wanted you turnin' vigilante killer. Not at your age anyway,' he muttered.

The short homily carried with the howl of the wind and Link didn't break the ensuing silence. A long while later, he heard Bose mumbling, grousing in his sleep. He began to understand a bit more. Bose hadn't simply led them back to a desert grave. He was there to try and prevent Link from going up against the killers when he found them.

3

Street Fight

Bose grinned, dug his knuckles into Link's side as they moved off from reading the notices outside the Albuquerque telegraph office.

'We ain't got a mention, Link,' he said. 'We must be doin' somethin' right.'

'You can't get into much trouble doin' nothin',' Link answered intolerantly.

It had been three years since they'd camped beside the grave of Elias Sawle. In that time a resolute friendship had developed between the boy and the old wrangler. But as time appeared to have slowed the ageing of Bose, so it had changed Link. Now he looked, acted older than his seventeen years.

'You know what day this is?' Bose asked him.

'I know it's March.'

'What time o' day then?'

Link looked at the silver, stem-winder that Bose had given him. ''Half past seven. Time we had supper,' he said.

'Suppose we bend an elbow, before we eat?' Bose suggested.

The two men stopped outside the Hundred Candles saloon. A thin man with long dark hair pushed out through the swing-doors, almost ran into them. Link felt Bose's left hand grip his arm, saw his right hand drop to the butt of his Colt .45 Peacemaker.

For a second, Bose and the man stared at each other. But then Bose and Link were through the doors, into the bar-room.

'Who was that?' Link immediately wanted to know.

'Never seen him before in my life . . . just bein' careful,' Bose said.

Link knew that wasn't the truth, and it offended him. But his thoughts were sidetracked when Bose raised an arm, greeted a tough-looking range man.

'Link,' he said, 'meet the best damned cowman that ever took a herd out of Texas. This here's Gilmer Crick of the Rollin' Wheel.' Bose held his hand towards Link. 'Gil, this is Link. His pa's Elias Sawle of Bear Ranch.'

'The hell it is,' said Crick, and offered to shake hands. 'I knew your pa well enough, kid. He was an interestin' man to do business with. Heard he took a bullet out on the Plain.'

'He took it in his back,' Link retorted.

'It was about the time a Pool herd headed for Cimarron got lost ... somewhere near Beck's Landin'. You remember that?' Bose asked.

'Yeah, I remember . . . got reason to,' Crick said with obvious bad feeling.

Bose was interested. 'Didn't know there was any Rollin' Wheel cattle in that herd,' he said.

'There wasn't,' Crick snapped back. His look stalled any further question, and Link saw Bose nod slightly, wink as the two men looked at each other.

'What you doin' here in Albuquerque?' Bose asked.

'I'm takin' a herd up to Wyoming . . . lookin' for good men,' Crick said.

'If you want me, you'll be wantin' the kid, an' it'll be for top dollar,' Bose demanded.

'Nothin' less,' Crick grinned agreeably.

'Me an' Link just got into town, an' I got me a hand or two to play. We'll catch you up. Where'll you be in four, five days from now?'

Crick looked shrewdly at Link, back to Bose. 'Raton. I'll be hirin' a crew, somewhere along the Canadian. Expect to be there a week,' he said.

★ ★ ★

For fifty cents, chilli-and-corn dodgers were being plated up from the end of the bar counter. Link and Bose took a full serving each, and with two beers they sat at a corner table. Not for the

18

first time, Link noticed that Bose placed his chair against a wall. It was so he could make out most, if not all, of what happened around him.

Link knew that Bose was a little uneasy, could see it in his wary, restless eyes. Nowhere west of the Texas line, did the old cowhand have a saintly reputation. Before settling down at Bear Ranch he'd been a man who'd ridden with all brands of men. Even in the last three years, Link knew there'd been occasions when they'd bedded down with an outlaw camp. But it wasn't Link's way to ask questions. He wouldn't judge Bose or any other man. He'd already learned to mind his own affairs, to ride swing on trouble.

They were spooning the last of their chilli, when a group of half a dozen men walked into the saloon. Two of them carried sawed-off shotguns and two more made a study of every man in the room. One of the two out front said something behind his hand and the other nodded.

Link sensed Bose's unease, noticed he kept both hands in plain sight on the edge of the table. Link thought the men looked like peace officers; from what tales he'd heard, Texas Rangers even. He took off his hat and ran his fingers through his curly, corn-coloured hair. He grinned at the one who seemed to be the leader.

'Evenin',' he said, tentatively.

The man returned the greeting, but without expression. Then he turned and walked away. The others followed, leaving the saloon as brusquely as they had entered.

Bose drained his beer-glass and wiped his moustaches with the back of his hand.

'I know him as Mr Silver,' he said, quiet and thoughtful. 'I reckon that's how most folk hereabouts know him. A few years back he offered me a room for the night; a room without convenience, so to speak.'

'He's the law in Albuquerque, is he?' Link asked.

Bose sniffed. 'Yeah. They call 'emselves 'The Committee of Vigilance' . . . or some such like. But Mr Silver's the law all right. Here, let me finish that good gravy, son,' he said, reaching for Link's plate.

* * *

Even though Bose was watchful tense, he was looking the wrong way. It was Link who saw the man standing in the street outside the saloon. There was no time to give warning. The man shouted something incomprehensible, then started firing.

Link swore, pulled his Colt and fired as fast as he could. He tried to recall everything Bose had taught him, but there in the dark street, it meant nothing. He was fearful, thrilled at the same time and he fired twice. The first heavy bullet smashed the man's knee-cap, the second ripped into his upper arm. The man managed to pull the trigger once more and a chunk of clapboard was torn out from behind Link's head. Link yelled, moved sideways as the man crashed through the pole hitching rail. As the man's face broke against the low step, Link hoped that he was avenging the death of his pa. He swore again, put a third bullet into the nape of the man's neck.

Bose was down on one knee, cradling a Sharps rifle in the crook of his arm. He was aiming coolly, shooting at three other men who were breaking up across the street. One of them threw up his arms and staggered backwards. With a bullet in his chest his body arched and he fell violently to the ground. The second had made it to his horse, was pulling himself into the saddle when he was hit. He dropped his gun to the dirt and grabbed the horn of his saddle. The horse squealed and kicked, pulled from its tether and whirled away.

Although the man was badly wounded, he'd got a foot into a stirrup. But the horse was frightened beyond control, and it bolted, dragging the man across the hard-packed dirt, his body struggling as it rolled and twisted.

Link watched as the man's foot came out of the stirrup, cursed holy blights on the world as the horse threw its head and galloped into the night.

Bose stared hard, levelled his sights at the third man, who was making a run for it. In the yellow light that glimmered from one or two windows along the street, Link saw the ashen face, recognized the thin man with the long, dark hair who'd almost run into them outside the Hundred Candles saloon.

The man turned into a narrow, dark alley and Bose held his fire, turned to Link and grunted with hard-faced satisfaction. He rose stiffly and grabbed Link's arm, pushed him into the crowd that was gathering along the boardwalk.

The town was in the deep shadow of night, and there was no one save Link and Bose who'd grasped what had actually happened. The shoot-out was so quick, and unexpected, that their identities were lost in the turmoil. They shoved their way through a shocked clutch of men, made their way into the safety of the darkness.

Towards the end of the street, Bose stopped them and they listened for a few seconds. He reloaded his gun, reminded Link to do the same.

'You did good kid,' he said quietly. 'But I thought I taught you to close-group your lead, not spread it around.'

Link grinned. 'Sorry Bose. Guess I got a little excited about savin' someone's hide.'

Bose grunted again, coughed at the irony. 'All that excitement's made me drier'n a lizard's butt. I'm goin' to get me a bottle,' he said gruffly. 'You get yourself to the horses an' wait. If I don't show up in thirty minutes . . . ride out. You hear me?'

Link pushed his reloaded gun back in its holster, puffed out his cheeks. 'Nothin' doin' Bose. We're partners an' I'm stayin' — ' he started.

24

'Yeah, but we ain't equal ones . . . not yet anyway,' Bose interrupted. 'If we're to meet Crick up on the Canadian, these ol' bones o' mine need their oil. Now, mind them horses.' With that, Bose was gone before Link could argue his case.

4

The Rolling Wheel Horses

From the bright arbour where he'd tethered their horses, Link became uneasy. As the long minutes ticked by, he struck a match to read his watch.

He knew that whiskey was Bose's greatest weakness. Usually the man wouldn't stop until he was well roostered, and sometimes the drink made him brash, too hasty.

Just after eleven o'clock, Link mounted his mare, walked it slowly up the street. In front of the telegraph office he reined in, looked over the small gathered crowd. He hoped he'd see Bose, but saw Gilmer Crick jawing with some cowboys. He dismounted, led the horse across the street to the Texas trail-boss.

'I'm lookin' for Bose. We had

ourselves a bit o' trouble,' he said warily. 'Now I don't know where he is.'

Crick half smiled. 'Mr Silver knows, him an' his vigilantes. We been lookin' out for you, kid . . . thought maybe they'd snatched you too.'

Before Link could ask him what he meant, Crick and the men were unhitching their horses.

'Go get the old ranny's mount,' Crick told Link. 'Meet us at the end o' town an' keep yourself hidden.'

It seemed like hours that Link waited in the spooky darkness for Crick to ride back. Gophers were scurrying beneath the shack and he flinched at the sound. There was very little moon and Link strained to see through the blackness. His ears had started to ring, when he heard the pummel of hoofs. Then he saw the group of men riding towards him. Crick was ahead of the cowboys, and Bose was riding with one of them. They slithered to a halt and Bose almost fell to the ground. He grabbed the reins of his own horse from Link and with a couple of loud, meaningful groans, pulled himself into the saddle.

'I'm obliged to you, Gil. See you along the Canadian,' he rasped.

The Rolling Wheel men wheeled their horses to face the town, as Crick waved farewell. Spirited and out of harm's way, Bose and Link kicked heels — hauled out towards Raton.

* * *

They'd covered more than five miles before Bose indicated for them to slow. He made quiet laughter as he pulled a flat bottle of White Mule from inside his jacket. He took a long pull, took a deep breath, then another pull.

'Goddamn lawless town. What sort of place calls itself *Albuquerque*?' he complained. 'From now on, Link, me an' you do our business elsewhere.' He glanced at Link from under the slanted brim of his hat. 'I told you to hightail it, if I didn't show,' he growled.

'I guess that old timepiece you gave

me must be runnin' slow,' Link said. What he really wanted to know was why four men had been waiting for them in the street. He wanted to know who the man with long, dark hair was. But as Bose drained his tequila, he guessed the answer to that would have to wait.

Many times in the last three years, Link had cared for Bose, got him through a bout of bottle fever, sobered him up on strong black coffee laced with chilli and gunpowder.

It wasn't until noon the day following, that Bose got through his drunk. Then another full day for him to recover, get some of his life-force back. He had a 'head' on him still, and was of a tremble, but that night he once more rode ahead. He reckoned there was a two-hundred-mile ride before they gathered with the Rolling Wheel herd.

To avoid renegades and desert *bandidos*, they rode at night, hid out during the day. Link estimated they'd travelled half that distance and it was approaching first dark when from a low, isolated mesa he sighted a bunch of horses, moving south.

'How many do you reckon, kid?' Bose asked.

'Fifty . . . sixty head. Three riders.'

Bose sat very still, stared thoughtfully into the distance. 'Well, they ain't Injun . . . not enough of 'em. An' if that's a dust-storm, they're movin' too fast. I reckon we got ourselves some horse-thieves, Link, and, unless we melt into this sand, they'll be ridin' right over us.'

The two men dismounted and bull-dogged their horses. They lay flat, hidden by snake weed and the shimmer off the sand.

'I know one o' them horses . . . the big, grey cloud-watcher,' Bose said after a few minutes of quiet waiting. He pulled his neck-cloth up around his nose, shielded his eyes from the sand that scudded around the bottom of the mesa. 'I can't see much Link, but I'd swear it's from Rollin' Wheel.'

'They'll be on top of us in less than five minutes. You'll be able to ask 'em,'

Link said quietly.

'Move back.' Bose nodded towards the far side of the mesa. 'The horses'll stay down. We'll pinch 'em from both sides. Don't poke your head up, you'll see 'em soon enough.'

'What we doin'?' Link asked guilelessly.

'Takin' back those horses. Don't you fire unless I do. You hear me, Link? This time, I want you to do what I say. I'll give 'em a chance,' Bose said, pulling his old big fifty from behind his saddle.

'Yeah, I'm sure you will,' Link muttered. In Albuquerque, he'd seen Bose coolly face up to four armed men. He wasn't about to question the general meaning of 'chance'.

In the lee of the mesa, where it broke into the desert floor, tumbleweed clumped, and Link crawled towards it. He stared into the last of the day's light, saw one man out front of the small herd. The two other riders were driving the horses behind him.

In the fading light, and though the

distance was over a hundred yards, Link recognized the man on the buck-skin mare riding point. He was wearing a dark, flat-brimmed hat and a faded duster, but it was unmistakably the thin man with long, black hair, from Albuquerque. Link never did get around to asking about the man's identity, and Bose had avoided telling.

Now, from sixty feet away, Link heard the boom of his friend's rifle. He looked out at the leading rider, saw him drag on his reins with one hand, snatch at his gun with the other.

Bose's voice immediately rasped through the echo of the warning shot.

'Hold up, Kerlue. This here Sharps is a .50 calibre. One bullet'll put you on top o' the Cristos, if I aim it proper. We're about to take back them branded horses an' we don't want any killin', so leave your guns alone.'

The long-haired man, the man Bose had called Kerlue, was peering ahead at the low mesa. He was tense, undecided, opened and closed his hand against the butt of his .44 Colt. Then Bose called out again.

'Link. Put a round over that son of a bitch's head.'

Link was levelling up a Winchester. There was just enough light to see Kerlue's hat through the sights and he was a fair shot.

Kerlue felt the bullet, the thudding pulse as if tore past his ear. It muffled Bose's abrasive laugh that followed from the other end of the mesa.

'The boy's a lot better'n me, Kerlue . . . reckon you seen that already. He could take out your eye if he'd a mind. Now, you goin' to leave them Rollin' Wheel horses, or is it wolf meat you're after bein'?'

Link waited for a response. He shivered at the situation, as the evening chill began to take hold. He levered another bullet into the chamber of his rifle.

'It's your hand, Bose, you drunken snake,' Kerlue yelled back. 'Let the horses go, Boone. The old *borracho*'s only winnin' small battles. Let's ride.'

'Stay where you are, Kerlue. I ain't a vindictive man, but I ain't stupid either.' Bose stood up, pointed the Sharps rifle at the horse-thief. 'You all toss down your saddle guns, an' bunch up. Move it.'

Link moved into the open, took a couple of paces until the men saw him. He jerked his rifle and the men dropped their guns to the ground.

'Good. Now, get down,' he said, picking upon Bose's intention. 'Turn your horses loose. You,' he added, looking at the man called Kerlue. 'You stay mounted. Mess up, an' you'll be nothin' more'n bleached bones in a week.'

Kerlue almost smiled. 'You ain't goin' to leave us with just my buckskin are you? We'll never make it.'

'You can take turn about. If the others don't like it, they can fight you for it.' Bose spat dryly into the sand. 'If the bad un's find you, they'll be savin' Mr Silver an' his vigilantes the trouble of hangin'. You best travel by night, so get movin'. Link,' he then called out. 'Come an' get the mare o' yours up. I reckon it's fallen asleep.'

Five minutes later, Link gathered the loose horses as they drifted around the mesa. He bunched them and they milled easy and contented. Darkness had already enveloped the three men who'd begun their long walk south as Bose rode alongside Link.

'We'll probably regret not shootin' them vultures off their perches,' he said thoughtfully. 'As long as that man's breathin', he's real dangerous. You ever hear of Dog Kerlue, kid?'

'I heard the name before. He must be some bad *hombre*. It was him that — '

'That tried to shoot us up in Albuquerque,' Bose cut in.

'You goin' to tell me about him, Bose?'

'Yeah, though there ain't a lot to tell. It was him that was movin' that Texas Pool herd. I *was* goin' to tell you, Link. I reckon Kerlue knows by now that you're Elias Sawle's kid. Like as not, he's the one who knows what happened to your pa.' Bose shot a quick glance at Link. 'But you ain't goin' after him now. We're takin' these shave-tails back to the Canadian.'

The whites of Link's eyes were shining in the dark as Bose sidled his horse up close.

'Remember, Link,' he said. 'Vengeance is somethin' best savoured cold.'

5

A Hanging Tree

They kept the horses moving all night, and in the morning they camped alongside fast-running water. Slumped in his saddle, Link was idly watching the graze while Bose slept. They'd take it in turns until dusk, then they'd be on the move again.

Link was drifting in and out of his own light sleep, when six armed men rode in on sweat-marked horses. At the time, Link's mind was lazy, wasn't ready for bad things. The men came close, with lowered rifles had the drop on him. Their mounts all carried the Rolling Wheel brand, and a thin sallow-faced rider appeared to be their leader. The man indicated for his men to cover Bose.

'Make a move for that gun, kid, an'

I'll put some bullets in yer belly,' he said, glaring malevolently. 'This place ain't no good for a hangin', what with no trees an' all. I guess you ain't got it *all* bad,' he then sniggered. He watched while Bose rolled on to his side, swearing, fumbling for his gunbelt. 'Take it easy Bose,' he advised him, then turned to one of his men. 'Take Lash an' Pully. Go back two or three miles, see if there's any more o' these horse-thieves. If there is, kill 'em.'

Bose shouted, rammed his hat on his head and started coughing. One or two of the Rolling Wheel hands recognized him and jeered.

'Caught you with yer pants down this time,' the leader called out. 'It's a real bad start to the day for you an' yer young friend.'

Bose grimaced, spat into the dirt. 'We never stole these horses, an' you know it Frost,' he grated. 'You think if we'd o' stolen 'em, we'd be ridin' back here to meet you, you dung brain? You best put off any thoughts of findin' a hangin'

38

tree 'til Crick gets here.'

'Take their guns,' Frost snapped. 'An' don't let the old *borracho* talk you out of it. Get him up on his horse an' tie his hands. We'll give 'em a real fine send-off from the first tree along the Canadian. Mr Crick can pay his respects if he happens to ride this way.'

'Someone else you forgot to tell me about?' Link mocked, as he and Bose were being tied in to their saddles.

'You don't carry that sort around in your head son,' Bose replied. 'Marlo Frost's a mean son of a bitch; but more worrying . . . he's actually some shirt-tail cousin of Gil Cricks. Just do what he says Link . . . say nothin'. Let's hope Gil knows how to deal with him when he gets here.' Bose turned back to Frost and shouted:

'Hey, Frost! You'll never see trees along the Canadian or any other river if you harm the kid.'

Frost wheeled his horse in a complete circle. He sneered at Bose. 'When Gil ain't here, I'm the ramrod o' this outfit. When an' if he gets here, you won't be doin' any complainin'. We'll have hung you already.'

★ ★ ★

It was only because there was no tree within fifty miles that Link and Bose lived to see another sunrise. Unless you were an Apache, it was customary to be hanged if you were a horse-thief, and most cowmen were superstitious, strong on tradition. The following day they rested for longer than usual. Three of the Rolling Wheel riders had been in the saddle for two days and nights. They'd ridden hard in their futile search for more horse-thieves. On their return, they half believed Bose's story that he and Link had taken the stolen horses away from Dog Kerlue.

'Naagh. Even Dog ain't that stupid,' Frost said. 'It was Bose an' the kid ran off them horses. Let's ride. We'll reach trees by sundown.'

As Marlo Frost tested the knots that

tied in Bose's wrists to the saddle-horn, Bose nodded toward the skyline. 'Them's Comancheros, Frost. Worse than Apache. If they've seen our dust, we'll be damned lucky if *any* of us live to see them cottonwoods. They'll take everythin'; includin' our skins. You'd better untie us, hand us back our guns.'

Frost didn't reply. Gilmer Crick had gone to Albuquerque and left him in charge of the outfit. He knew it was only Comancheros who would be confident enough to ride the skyline and it worried him.

Bose saw the hesitation, the confused look, and followed his advantage.

'Me and Link would o' been sighted by 'em. You showin' up unexpected, maybe kept 'em from attackin' us. But now they'll attack as soon as dark comes. Maybe before, if there's enough of 'em. Either way, they'll get so close you'll be smellin' 'em, before you see 'em,' he threatened. 'Now make sure these knots are real tight, if you reckon it'll help your chances to live.'

Frost scowled, climbed on to his horse and rode to check the remuda. He left Bose and Link with the two men who were going to lead them off.

Bose chortled. 'When them mongrels chew the feathers from that bird, you'll get to hear him squawkin',' Bose chortled.

'If we was to untie you and the kid, give you your guns, what would you do?' one of the Rolling Wheel men asked anxiously.

'I'd be sorely tempted to put a few holes in Marlo Frost . . . and maybe you along with him,' admitted Bose. 'But if any of us want to make the Canadian, we'll likely need all the ironware we can muster. There's a goddamn big bunch of Comancheros out there.'

'What would you really do?' the man asked again.

Bose smiled grimly. 'Stop us movin' . . . hold the horses in real tight. If we let the dust settle, there's a chance

. . . just a chance, them scalpers won't see us.'

'I ain't for gettin' caught,' the man said, his eyes flitting to the horizon. 'I hear they eat your ears.'

'Only if they like you,' Bose told him. 'You go talk to your boss. See if you can change his mind.'

Within five minutes, Frost was riding alongside Bose. 'What you been scarin' Minnow with?' he snarled.

'The truth. Listen, Frost,' Bose snapped back at him. 'Maybe your body parts ain't up to much, but most o' mine are. If you want to hang on to what you got 'til mornin', get us dug in to this river, quick. Let those Coman-cheros move on to wherever they're goin'.'

Frost chewed his lip, thought of the alternative. Then he nodded to the men who'd been listening up. 'Set yer pieces and keep quiet,' he said. 'But if either of these horse-thieves makes a move, shoot 'em. We'll take our chances.'

Three men looped in the small herd,

nervously held them steady along the river. The others crouched with guns ready under the shelving bankside. Frost cursed at a high-circling buzzard, damned it for having noted their inactivity.

For many hours they waited, chewed on jerked beef until the last of the day's heat evaporated. The men shivered at the chill, then later at the wind in the mesquite. Long before midnight, the tension got to Frost.

'We're movin' out,' he hissed. 'I'd rather face them dogs in the open . . . see the yellow o' their eyes.'

Some of the men turned to Bose's huddled form, waited for his reaction.

'I doubt you'll be doin' that,' he said. 'I reckon they're half-way to the Tongue River by now.'

'Why'd you not say earlier?' Frost demanded.

'Wanted to be sure. Keep us all alive a bit longer. Thought maybe you'd lift the death penalty.'

Bose and Link rode well behind point

of the small herd. They were moving north and west, towards where they'd first spotted the Comancheros. There was little moonlight, but they knew it was Frost who approached them. The man gave Link a strange grin.

'I been thinkin',' he said. 'Could be I owe you two for somethin'. I'll owe you the hangin'. But if you're still around after fillin' yer bellies, I'll paint the sand with yer blood. You graspin' that?'

'Tightly,' said Bose, with a sharp nod.

Frost and the two men with him rode on and Bose made a twisted grin.

'Don't reckon we'll be goin' up the trail with the Rollin' Wheel herd, son. Even if Gil believes our story . . . still wants us to ride with him, we can't go. Him an' Frost are kin. There'll be whittle-whangin' an' sides to choose. There's other herds trailin' to Fort Collins or Cheyenne. We'll hire out to one of 'em. Horse-thieves can't cherry-pick, Link, an' I reckon some o' my unsavoury ways have rubbed off on you. We'll go to Pueblo. After that, you'll be a heap better off goin' it alone. Trailin' with crow-bait like me ain't gettin' you far off the trail.'

'You loaded up again, Bose, with that defeatist talk? We're goin' together, or not at all.' Link sounded genuinely hurt-angered.

Under the brim of his battered hat, a smile softened Bose's weather-beaten face. 'Somethin' I meant to tell you,' he said, as they rode along behind the horses. 'Back in Albuquerque . . . fightin' in the street. You reminded me of your pa.'

'In what way?'

'Oh I don't know. You ain't got enough years on you for anythin' certain.'

They rode in silence for a while. Link thought that Bose was going to tell him something about his father, sensed there was something being held back.

'Did Elias ever tell you about your ma?' Bose asked, in time.

'No. He never did.'

Bose shook his head sadly. 'She was a

fine woman, Link. The only real wrong your pa ever did, was leavin' her on her own for too long . . . too often.'

'Yeah, her an' me an' the brother I never knew,' Link said sourly and the silence returned.

An hour after daybreak, they first sighted the Canadian River. An hour after that, they dismounted wearily, watched as their horses sank their noses in the fast, cool-running water. Bose nodded at the big cotton-woods on the bank.

'If I had to be hung, Link, I'd like it to be from a cotton-wood. Better'n an oak or piñon or blackjack even,' he reflected.

Link chuckled. 'I'll bear that in mind, when you ask Frost for our guns back,' he said.

6

Bad Family

A week later, Bose and Link were in Pueblo. For nearly two hundred miles they'd worked their way north-east of the Rocky Mountains. They rode around Raton, hadn't lingered on the Canadian for Gilmer Crick. The Rolling Wheel camp didn't have a big enough spread for Bose and Marlo Frost to steer clear of each other's fists or guns.

Though Link said nothing to Bose, he had his own personal reasons for remembering Pueblo. It was here that he and Jackson had been taken once by their mother to visit their grandparents. His memory of the town was dim. He recognized none of the buildings of the sprawling cowtown, the rows of frame-buildings, saloons and wide plank sidewalks. But as he and Bose stabled their horses and walked down the street, half-forgotten memories crowded into his mind. Bose wouldn't notice his silence, the lack of interest in saloons and gambling-houses, and it troubled him because of it. Bose knew the story of Ruth Sawle's flight to Pueblo, so why didn't he say anything? To Link's way of thinking, other than drinking and gambling, Bose didn't say anything about other stuff . . . ever.

It was getting dark and lights were coming on along the main street. Link stopped outside of a hotel that had two peach trees out front. Frowning, he studied the painted sign: THE ORCHARD HOTEL. There'd been a bar and dining-room downstairs, he remembered, an office with a desk and a bell that you rang to summon the fat proprietor or his fat wife from the kitchen. Link took a deep breath, stepped inside trying to recall some-thing. He laughed at one memory. It was of his brother stabbing a pen back into a potato which had been atop the signing-in desk.

Link noticed that Bose had followed him, was standing inside the doorway quietly watching. He was about to say something about leaving, when a girl came down the narrow stairs that led to first-floor rooms. As Link stared at the first girl he'd seen in weeks, she approached him, spoke directly.

'You ring that bell?' The girl's eyes were almost as black as the hair that shone glossy under the big glass pendant-lamp. Her skin was tanned, not city white and her voice was soft and purry, but it made Link jump.

'No,' he spluttered uncertainly.

The girl, who was about Link's age, picked up on his embarrassment, went on talking as she stepped behind the reception desk.

'Just as well, there's no one to hear you,' she said. 'The only room that's available is directly above the bar. It's where the marshal puts his drinks . . . a corpse sometimes. The floor's full of holes from drunken cowboys. They call it the resting-place.'

She smiled and Link felt more at ease. He became aware of his appearance as he hauled off his hat. He stood dust-coated, with a few specks of dried blood across his shirt front. He carried a sprig of beard across his chin and his curly hair was sweat-pressed against his forehead. He stood there dumb, thanked a 'sweet Jesus' for the welcome sound of Bose's voice.

'You're that Texas mite from Sweetwater. Little Rachel Crick of the bare leg and cotton britches,' he was insisting.

The girl made a short breathless sound, then she was around the counter, hugging Bose, who chuckled, grinned at Link's gaze.

She was the only daughter of Gilmer Crick. Her mother had died giving birth, and she'd been wet-nursed, raised by nannies at the Sweetwater ranch. All this and many other things about her, Link was to learn later.

'Rachel, say hello to my young partner, Link Sawle. He ain't normally as dumb as he looks right now. But you'd unsettle any colt, showin' up bright as a summer poppy.' Bose winked at Link. 'Meet Rachel Crick,' he said. 'Gil's young 'un. What in tarnation you doin' in Pueblo?' he then asked her.

'Waitin' for Dad. They're driving the Rollin' Wheel herd . . . comin' through Raton. Didn't you come up with 'em?'

'Not exactly,' Bose laughed to himself. 'But we seen him in Albuquerque . . . chirpy as a meadow-lark. Me an' Link had to leave there pronto. We rode ahead.'

'Hmmm,' she said, almost without listening. 'We sold our ranch in Sweetwater . . . used the money to buy some Rollin' Wheel longhorns and horses. We're going into business for ourselves in Montana.' Rachel looked sharply at Bose. 'What's holding back the trail-herd, Bose? Has anything happened?'

Bose was caught for a second. He

was thinking — interested in what Rachel had just said about owning Rolling Wheel stock.

'Yeah . . . I mean no,' he said. 'The herd's comin' as quick as Gil catches up. They're laid over on the Canadian . . . fattenin' 'em up on tallow-weed.' Bose nodded towards Link. 'The kid's too polite to ask for his hand back,' he said mischievously.

Rachel said something under her breath, let go of Link's hand. She and Link looked at each other and laughed, the awkward reserve broken.

'You both come and see me, when you've done what you have to do,' she said. 'I'm worried about why Pa went to Albuquerque. It's a way off the trail. He never mentioned it to me. I wonder if it had anything to do with what happened to Uncle Jigger?'

'Shucks, young 'un. Your pa's safe enough,' Bose said, as sincerely as he could. 'He had four or five of the Rollin' Wheel boys with him. He's hirin' more men, an' ain't comin' to much harm doin' that.'

As he attempted to reassure Rachel, Bose saw Link twitching his nose at the warm aromas that drifted from the dining-room.

'Me an Link'll call on you when we've had our hair trimmed,' he said. 'We'll get into some clean duds . . . have a bath even, before we eat, ha, ha.'

* * *

Five minutes later Bose and Link were standing each other beers at the bar of the Sand 'n Sun saloon.

'Who's Uncle Jigger? What happened to him?' Link asked.

'Rachel's uncle . . . Gil's brother. He started off with that Texas herd. But somethin' must o' happened on the trail. He never was heard of again. Jigger was a well-turned-out *hombre* . . . tough. Over the years he put some grey hair on Gil's head, I can tell you. But you could ride the river with him.'

'Was he among the dead you buried? Those that got burned near Beck's Landin'?' Link wanted to know. It was a direct question, one that Bose was expecting.

'I told you they'd been dead some time when I found 'em. The buzzards and coyotes had done their grisly work. You want me to spell it out, Link?'

Link felt that while Bose was telling him the truth about what had happened, there was something evasive, something missing, something about Jigger Crick. And he didn't remind Bose of the remark he'd made the day he led him to the spot where the Texas Pool outfit had been slaughtered. Bose had said then that he'd know the ones that got away. Link knew instinctively the men they'd killed back in Albuquerque had been mixed up in the killing, as had Dog Kerlue. Bose had said that much, but he'd never mentioned any brother of Gil's. Link also remembered the curious, scheming look that had passed between Gil Crick and Bose that

55

night in the Hundred Candles.

Bose broke up Link's train of thought then. 'I'm wonderin' about that herd . . . an' the horses,' he said. 'I never knew they belonged to Gil. So, I'm wonderin' who else knew.'

'Howd's it matter?' Link asked.

'Dog Kerlue ain't stupid enough to go raidin' anythin' that belonged to Rollin' Wheel. They're too big . . . too powerful a set-up. They'd hunt him down.' Bose scratched his chin. 'No, son, Gil never told anyone that the herd was his, that it was honestly bought from Rollin' Wheel. It would've been too risky. He wanted to stay safe . . . not end up like them Texas Pool herders. But sometime Kerlue got told of it. My guess is, it's a bad family thing.'

'The shirt-tail cousin, Marlo Frost?' Link suggested.

'Yeah, him. an' maybe . . . just maybe the sugar-sweet Rachel's in on it, too.'

Link whistled softly. 'An' her Uncle Jigger?'

'No, I don't think so. I reckon he's turnin' his toes in the daisies, somewhere.'

'You want I should keep an eye on the girl?'

'Yeah. But don't get too comfy or go soft on her. Get ready to leave town fast.'

'First, I'm goin' to get me that cleanin' up,' Link said. 'What *you* doin', need I ask?'

As Link turned away, Bose touched him on the arm. 'You hopin' to find trace of your ma?' he asked him kindly.

'My ma, an' my brother. I was hopin' . . . ' Link stopped as Bose shook his head.

'You won't, Link. Ruth went north from here,' he said. 'Just plumb disappeared.'

'How'd you know any of that?' Link asked.

'I been askin' questions for a long time. It's likely Jackson's still around though. We'll find out kid . . . one day. Now why don't you go get yourself prettied up . . . buy some new duds.'

* ★ *

Link pulled himself from the chair, smiled awkwardly at his reflection in the mirror. He nodded at the barber.

'Somewhere I could change into these?' he asked, looking to where he'd placed his bundle of new clothes. He saw they weren't on the wooden bench where he'd put them when he came in. 'Where's my bundle . . . my package?' Suddenly bothered, he looked around the barber's shop.

'I been busy lookin' after your locks young feller. Maybe you noticed,' the man who'd cut his hair said. 'Some sort o' romper set was it?'

One or two other men who were waiting sniggered, made a similar, wounding response.

Link smiled at the men. 'No, they was my new dude chaps . . . wool jacket'n pants. I was hoping to wear 'em . . . not lose 'em,' he said mildly serious to the barber. Then his face lost its colour as his strong, muscled fingers, gripped and twisted the barber's fancy white shirt. The feeling of being hurt returned and he slapped the man's face with the open flat of his hand, felt the sting in his fingers. 'You ain't funnin' at my expense, hair-cutter. Where'd you put my package?'

The barber blinked, blew hard. 'I ain't seen your package, kid. You're goin' to pay dearly for . . . '

As he spoke, Link smacked him in the face again. This time he made a fist, drew blood as the man's lip split open.

'I'm in need, an' I'm goin' to carry on hammerin' your face until my belongin's are returned. You understand, mister?' Link drew back his fist again.

'It's in the cupboard. I put it there.' One of the men waiting, stood up. 'We was just havin' a bit o' fun. Somethin' wrong with you, kid?' the man demanded angrily.

'I ain't got much of a sense of that,' Link said. 'This'll be from the barber.' With that, Link pushed the barber away, hit the man between the eyes. The immediate stab of pain exploded up his arm. He groaned, cursed, lunged after the second man who was half-way through the door. Link stepped out onto the boardwalk, kicked out at the man. He caught him behind his knees and the man buckled. He fell against a railing and Link heaved him over, pushed him down into the water-trough that ran along the front of the building.

'*That's* fun! Three grown men against an itty bitty kid's just aggravation,' Link mockingly exclaimed. He stepped back into the barber's shop and retrieved his parcel, flicked a coin among the bottles of pomade.

*   *   *

Less than five minutes later, in the Sun 'n Sand, Bose was listening to one version of the brawl.

'Yessir, we got our own champeen fighter. Calm an' cool as you like,' the man was saying. 'The kid took 'em on. Shavin' Sam an' two of his regulars. He tipped Neck Shippum into the horse-trough. No one's seen the youngster around these parts before, but he put a bit of excitement into the street.'

'This kid have long fair hair . . . curly?' Bose asked.

'Didn't look so long to me, but yeah, sounds like him.'

Bose spat into the big brass cuspidor. 'His name's Link,' he chuckled. 'There's a lot o' folk he don't like. Me an' him are partners.'

By a curious twist of fate, Link Sawle had created himself a little notoriety. For a few roused townsfolk in and about Sun 'n Sand saloon, he'd become the 'game-cock.'

7

The Boy Wales

At the end of town, Bose and Link stood in an empty feed-stall, screwed up their noses at the smell of horse sweat and damp straw.

'No Link, it ain't that I'm troubled by stiffs,' explained Bose, as they spread their blankets. 'But sleepin' in the same room? Anyways they're strangers . . . an' probably carryin' a whiff. Here's good enough for me.' He took a long pull from the bottle he'd brought from the Sun 'n Sand, looked at Link. 'You wear them duds like you growed into 'em, kid. Most fellers in that rig would look like a mule peerin' over a whitewashed fence. They store-bought?'

Link nodded. 'Yeah. They belonged to a tinhorn . . . got himself killed last week. He was about my size, an' the storeman let me have 'em discounted. His missus patched up the bullet-hole real good. Even his boots and hat was my fit. They're tailor-made, Bose . . . homespun.'

Bose grinned, didn't dare say the town was already calling him 'game-cock'.

'By the way,' Link said. 'I think I saw Dog Kerlue earlier on.'

'Dog Kerlue . . . you certain? Pueblo's way off his track.'

'I could've been mistaken . . . didn't get a good look at him. The light was dim down the street, he was with three, maybe four, other riders. They pulled off the main street, I didn't see 'em again. There was somethin' about one of 'em, though . . . wore a funny hat . . . city-like. You know of anyone like that, Bose?'

Bose took off his own hat. He thought for a moment, scratched the top of his head. 'Well if it's who I think it is, I wouldn't o' thought he'd be mixed up with the likes o' Kerlue, an' it'd make for two of 'em out o' their territory. The hat's called a derby. You ever hear tell o' Boy Wales, Link?'

Link nodded in the darkness. 'Yeah. I heard. The kids at school had some stories. You reckon that was him?'

'Could've been. I've never sighted him close . . . not many have. They claim he don't use a gun . . . throws a bolas. But it's possible it was him, Link.'

In the darkness, Link caught a faltering measure in Bose's voice, as though he was moving through a recollection.

'If it *is* Kerlue, I'll find him,' Bose went on. 'And maybe we'll find out somethin' of Wales at the same time.' He looked brightly at Link. 'Suddenly I don't feel so tired. Let's go find 'em.'

* * *

But if Dog Kerlue or the infamous Boy Wales were in Pueblo, they were keeping well hidden. Link and Bose searched until first light. Bose prodded at barkeeps, dance-hall girls, gamblers, drifting cowboys. But although he'd been heard of, nobody had seen Kerlue. As for Boy Wales? He'd never been seen in Pueblo. Most folk thought that he moved in and out of Colorado Springs.

The two men went about their search quietly and methodically. Bose managed to keep their enquiries from the eyes and ears of the town's tough, diligent law officers.

They'd slept until noon, were now standing in the main street under the full sun, considering food.

'To think my ma brought Jackson back here,' Link said. 'God knows whatever became of 'em, Bose. There's no trace of Ma's family any more.'

Bose's curious behaviour returned. He merely grunted a response, and Link said no more.

★   ★   ★

It was the same day some time after full dark, when news came to town that Gilmer Crick had been killed.

A man who was jumpy and scared was talking his head off in the saloon where interested parties had gathered.

'No, I never seen it,' he was saying. 'I jus' got the message to give Crick's gettin' dust in his beard somewhere between Albuquerque and the Rollin' Wheel camp. Shove a gun into the gut of a horse-thief named Bose Marshfield and he'll lead you there.'

'Is that it?' someone asked without prejudice.

'That's the meat of it, yeah. Someone's to tell his daughter, she don't have to wait. Don't have to stay in Pueblo any longer.'

Link moved, but Bose held up his hand to stop him. 'I know it's hard, son, but you had schoolin'. They learn you not to shoot the messenger?' He looked hard at the marshal, who nodded.

'That'd be my advice too, son,' he warned. 'An' it won't change the truth of it. I've already sent two deputies to the Rollin' Wheel camp. They'll fetch back proof of Crick's death . . . if there is any. I'm interested to know what's behind all this.'

'Well, there'll be some sort of frame-up that I killed him,' Bose offered. 'And what are the chances of that *proof* implicatin' young Link here, Marshal?'

The marshal gave a thin smile. 'As I said, I'm interested to know what's goin' on. There's goin' to be a load o' wild talk, an' the Rollin' Wheel outfit'll be my town. No doubt some of those boys thought a lot of Gilmer Crick.'

Link had been thinking. 'When are we supposed to have done this?' he asked keenly.

'Sometime between when you left camp on the Canadian and when you got here. It would've been after you'd got your guns back, I guess,' the marshal said.

'Yeah, from Marlo Frost. Now you're givin' us a chance to hightail it if I hear you right,' Bose speculated.

The marshal shrugged, gave a regretful look. 'Might be just as well if you slipped out o' town. Stayin' here would only mean trouble. Town's buryin' the Ruggles girl tomorrow at noon. Go then. No one'll notice.'

'Yeah, we'll do that, Marshal.' Bose turned to Link. 'Find Rachel,' he said. 'Make sure no one gets to her with news of her pa. Try and convince her you weren't mixed up in any bushwhack killin'.'

★　★　★

For a few moments, Link shuffled his feet, then he knocked. Rachel opened the door slowly, stood blinking for a moment in the hall light.

'Sorry,' he said. 'I know it's late. Just checkin' that you're OK.'

'Thank you. That's very thoughtful . . . timely too. Somebody *did* try my door . . . earlier. I must've just fallen asleep. There was the usual town noises

... they don't keep me awake any more. But for some reason I'd left the lamp on ... turned low. Now and then a drunken cowboy finds his way up the stairs. I can hear them fumbling around in the hallway. But the man who tried my door was sober enough ... didn't make any noise.'

'How'd you know he was there then?' Link asked smartly.

'One of his boots ... it squeaked. It was the unusual noise that woke me. I'd bolted the door, but I saw the handle turn.'

'You must've been real worried ... frightened.'

'It would take a lot more than that, Link. No, I was wondering if he'd been doing *that* if he'd known I had Pa's scattergun covering the door.' Rachel smiled broadly and Link had a reserved laugh.

'Yeah, well, as I said, I just came to see you were all right. I guess I can go now.'

'I don't know who you think's likely

to harm me, Link, but thank you anyway.' Rachel winked. 'Do *your* boots squeak?' she asked playfully as she pushed the door to, quietly.

'That would've been the son of a bitch who brought news of Gil Crick's death, I reckon,' Link muttered to himself as he went back down the stairs of the Orchard Hotel.

8

In and Out of Pueblo

Link spent most of the following morning in the Orchard Hotel with Rachel. They played cards, and Link talked. He talked more than he'd ever talked before because he knew that, in a few hours, Rachel's world would be shadowed by grief. He'd never met, let alone spoken with many girls, and she knew it, took advantage of his reserve.

When Bose came to get Link, Rachel wanted to come along too, but Bose said no. He wouldn't take on the responsibility, wanted her to stay in town within the protection of the marshal's office.

They climbed into their saddles, moved out of the livery stable. It was midday, and Pueblo was busy. A lot of the townsfolk were attending the popular Annie Ruggles's funeral, didn't notice the two men quietly leaving town. As they turned their horses west, Bose spoke in a thoughtful, quiet voice.

'I'll bet my liver that news of Gil Crick's death has been spread around . . . that you an' me are mixed up in it. The game's on, Link, we'll have to breathe shallow.'

They rode far beyond the edge of town, in and out of the trees along the Arkansas River. They found cover in the deep shade and dismounted.

'You an' Rachel get to know each other, son?' Bose asked.

Link's face coloured with raw feeling. 'Yeah, I got to like her,' he said.

Bose was watching his horse at the water's edge. 'She's a good girl . . . always was. I've known her since she was a yearlin'. She ain't the kind o' kid to get mixed up in this business.'

'What happens next, Bose?' Link wanted to know.

'Before either of us are much older, Marlo Frost will be in Pueblo. He'll be tellin' how Gil Crick's been bush-whacked somewhere out of Albuquerque. He's goin' to swear it was you an' me done it. He's got a blood-line through to Rachel, so he'll be paintin' a real black picture. The family connection makes him her lawful guardian an' protector. We don't know how much of all that she'll believe, Link. I'm sure Frost can be mighty impressionable.'

The horse's bellies were full of water and Link eased their noses into the bankside sedge.

'Yeah, Bose, but tell me about the killin' an' what we're goin' to do about it,' he said impatiently.

Bose sat with his back against the bole of a stunt pine. He removed his hat, wiped his forehead before he answered.

'I think you've guessed that I know more'n I'm lettin' on, Link. I'm sorry for that, but there's a reason for it. I'll tell you what I can . . . what I reckon's happenin'. Listen good . . . see what

73

you can make of it.' Bose chewed on a short blade of grass as he carried on. 'It's to do with Dog Kerlue stealin' those Rollin' Wheel horses. There's somethin' queer about it. Frost wasn't expectin' to get 'em back, and he had his own reasons for wantin' you an' me strung up before Gil showed. Frost and Kerlue was partners in that deal, I know it. If Frost knowed them mounts belonged to Gil, then Kerlue knew it. I suggest we let 'em run their colours up the pole, Link.'

Link was squinting with concentration. 'I'm followin' . . . just about,' he said slowly, and Bose continued:

'For some reason Gil delayed the herd . . . took himself an' a few of his men to Albuquerque.'

'Why'd he do that?' Link asked.

'The only reason I can think of, is that he hoped to find his brother, Jigger, there. He liked Jigger, even though they was always arguin' . . . always headin' for a big fight. In the end, he ran him off Rollin' Wheel land at gunpoint. Gil took doin' that, real hard. I'm sure for some reason he thought Jigger was in Albuquerque . . . but he wasn't. He was in Colorado Springs. I reckon Gil was decoyed.' Bose saw the excitement in Link's eyes, saw him mouth the words 'Colorado Springs'.

'Yeah, that's right. Jigger weren't killed out at Beck's Landin'. He either got away or he was one of the rustlers. He rides with Boy Wales.'

Link was getting more curious. 'You think it *was* Boy Wales in Pueblo . . . with Dog Kerlue?' he wanted to know.

'That's my guess, Link. An' I'm guessin' further, that it was Kerlue had somethin' to do with gettin' Gil into Albuquerque. You remember the gunfight? Kerlue and his men was there to shoot Gil. We sort o' stuck their cards together. They must've seen us talkin' to Gil in the saloon . . . tried to take us in the street. Kerlue was lucky. I had the chance to put a bullet in him. That's when he headed for the Canadian. He managed to keep out o' sight o' the Rollin' Wheel boys ... talked it over with Marlo Frost.'

'What did he ... they want?' Link asked uncertainly.

'The remuda ... the herd maybe. But for some reason they didn't get it.'

'You reckon Jigger was part o' that?'

'Dunno for sure. They're as close as dogs an' fleas ... him an' Frost an' Kerlue. But Jigger weren't goin' to shoot his own brother, for Chrissake. An' if he *was* stealin' horses, he figured they belonged to the Rollin' Wheel, not Gil.'

'You think, Jigger was with Boy Wales and Dog Kerlue, then?'

'If he was in town, he'd o' been with Rachel. Jigger treasured his niece an' he would o' gone to see her ... but he didn't. The trouble is, Link, there's too many people knowin' too much.'

'Yeah,' said Link, and told Bose about the man with squeaky boots who'd tried Rachel's door.

Bose grunted his aggravation. 'Some-one's been informin' the marshal, too.' Bose stared up at Link. 'Just in case you was thinkin' of goin' back . . . you ain't. I agreed with the marshal we'd stay away from town,' he told him.

'I never said goodbye to Rachel.'

Bose swore. 'This side o' the Brazos, sayin' goodbye's often for the best,' he said enigmatically. 'Anyways, it's too big a risk. Frost and a lot of Rollin' Wheel men will have arrived. The whole town'll know about Gil. Kerlue's likely to be holed up somewhere, an' you ain't forgot how Marlo Frost looks forward to a neck-stretchin', have you?'

Link thought for a few seconds. There's one or two other things I should've told Rachel, he mused. Just reckon I'll have to ride back alone.

9

Campfire Story

Pueblo had two graveyards. One was Boot Hill, where they bury men — and the rare woman — who die with their boots on. The other was for the likes of Annie Ruggles and those who meet a less-violent death.

Link and Bose avoided both, rode into town cautiously from the south. From the cover of an alley-way they stopped for a moment, watched six men carry a coffin from one of the buildings into the street.

Marlo Frost and a dozen or more Rollin' Wheel cowboys had ridden into town. They'd brought with them the news that upheld the story of Gilmer Crick's death. They told of the horse-thief Bose Marshfield as the murderer, together with his young partner, Lincoln Sawle.

Pueblo gushed with stories, but the marshal was awaiting news from the Rolling Wheel camp. He remained calm and non-committal, spread the word that he'd only stand for a legal hanging. He spoke to a group of men who'd assembled outside the Sun 'n Sand saloon.

'Gil Crick was a friend of mine . . . a good friend,' he told them. 'No one's more keen than me to know the truth of his death. Any of you come up with a warrant for Marshfield an' Lincoln Sawle and I'll arrest 'em.' The marshal snapped the barrel of his rifle down against a hitching rail for effect. 'But take the law unto yourselves, even talk bad, an' I'll show you little mercy. You can tell that to Marlo Frost, wherever he may be.'

*   *   *

Frost was in Rachel Crick's room at the Orchard Hotel. He'd gone there after getting into town, straight after he'd learned that Link and Bose had disappeared. He'd wasted no time in breaking the tidings of her father's death.

'Bose Marshfield never killed my father, nor did Link,' Rachel insisted through the first incredible, aching stab of grief.

'I got the proof, Rachel. I blame myself for not hangin' the pair of 'em when I had the chance. Marshfield once trailed with Dog Kerlue. For the last two or three years, this young Link Sawle has been his partner. They would've hung him at Albuquerque, but he managed to get away.'

'No. I can't . . . I won't believe that they had anything to do with . . . with what you say.'

'If not, Rachel, why'd they scuttle, when they heard I was comin' in?'

'I don't think the two are connected. Maybe they just didn't want to be in the same town as you.' Glassy-eyed, Rachel stared down into the street.

'Now why don't you get out . . . leave me alone,' she said bitterly.

Frost cursed under his breath as Rachel pushed the door to, slammed in the bolt behind him. Driven by ugly temper he stomped downstairs, straight into the street. He'd been so sure of himself, so sure of being able to offer the comfort after inflicting the hurt. He'd been counting on it.

There must have been a reason for Rachel's reaction, and Frost rolled the whys and wherefores around in his head. What if Gil had hinted anything, back at Sweetwater. Might he have said anything to make his daughter suspicious? Tell her that there was no trust between the two men?

Hell no, it couldn't have been that. She'd known Marshfield a long time, was now going soft on young Link Sawle. Yeah, that'd be it. He'd have to dig up some sticking evidence. He went through what he'd got. The Rolling Wheel men had bought the story of Gilmer Crick. Dog Kerlue had done a good job there, despite a run of bad luck due to Marshfield and Sawle. But he was still ahead. They were Kerlue's men who'd been riding with Gil Crick — the real killers. They were the ones who'd sat around the Rollin' Wheel camp-fire and lied about the cold-blooded kill by Bose Marshfield and Lincoln Sawle.

Other than Kerlue and his hench-men, there was no one who knew the moment of Gil's death, no one who knew that Bose and Link were actually Marlo Frost's prisoners when it took place. With one horse between them, Kerlue and his two partners had been walking their way back to Albuquerque. There were cross-trails, but it was by chance they'd sighted Gil's camp-fire in the middle of the night. Gil Crick and his three trusty comrades were strangled. Knifed, then shot with their own guns to make sure.

The story that Kerlue and Frost had contrived had been iron-clad, no chance of a giveaway. To eliminate any chance of a slip-up, this time Frost was itching to have Bose and Link jerking a rope without delay. He was hoping that Link would have the nerve to show himself in town, him and his partner.

For the murderers of Gilmer Crick, the crowd would break from Annie Ruggles's funeral, put the Boot Hill to use. Frost swallowed hard, choked back the frustration. He needed a drink, but wasn't in the mood to mingle with a saloon crowd. He turned into an alleyway between two buildings on the main street, considered the door of a *pulqueria*.

As he was about to go in, a shadow bent across the narrow run and he turned nervously. It looked like a man was leading his horse to the end of the alleyway, away from the street. He swore silently as he flattened himself against the clapboards, watched aghast as the man mounted the horse, nudged it forward. It was only a brief glimpse, but was enough to leave Frost shaken as he pushed into the decrepit tavern. The man was Jigger Crick. The man who, only a week ago, Dog Kerlue had sworn was dead. As dead as his brother Gil.

Frost ordered a bottle of sotol, trembled as he poured himself a large glassful. He couldn't taste, almost choked as the liquid blistered his throat. He cursed his predicament. Kerlue had either lied, or been mistaken about Jigger Crick. The man was alive, and as such, a threat far more dangerous than Marshfield or Sawle.

Frost finished the bottle, paid one dollar for the pleasure. He was sick by the time he'd collected his horse, worse by the time he'd joined the Rolling Wheel cowboys who were milling restless at the end of town.

* * *

From the balcony of the Orchard Hotel, Rachel watched Annie Ruggles's coffin as it passed beneath her. She was still numb, dazed but angry. She wanted some space, something to lash out at.

She looked along the street, into shadows and doorways for a glimpse of Link. She saw the marshal standing on the boardwalk opposite, watching. Riding with his men, Marlo Frost glanced upwards towards her and she turned away. She waited until the street had cleared, saw no sign of the men she was looking for.

She went back into her room, and changed, put on flannel shirt, pants and riding-boots. She pushed her black hair under the high crown of a felt hat. She glanced in the mirror, saw the tanned, boylike image — man at a distance.

Rachel walked purposefully to the livery, quickly saddled a rented horse. With her hat-brim pulled low across her eyes, and a neck-cloth around her mouth and chin, only someone up close would see through the anonymity she wanted.

At the north end of the main street she sat off from the burial group. She gritted her teeth, closed her eyes for a moment, watched a little girl lay a bloom on top of Annie Ruggles's coffin.

There was still no sign of Bose or Link, but she saw that the marshal had joined the group. He sat a big bay mare, stared hard at the morose Frost, the Rolling Wheel cowboys who stayed bunched. Rachel caught a glimpse of Frost's face. It was greasy grey from the cheap booze.

The town barber was there with Neck Shippum. Both men were bruised, as well as half-drunk and armed. They'd made threats against Link and were waiting a chance to get even. It was all these men whom the marshal was watching closely.

'That kid ain't goin' to show,' he called to Frost.

'He'll be here. I'll bet on it.'

'What you goin' to make that wager with?' the barber wanted to know.

'My share o' the trail herd, an' the horses,' Frost said. But he hadn't meant to. It was the sotol doing the talking.

The barber laughed, unaware of the significance. Rachel sat her horse, her stomach churning. She turned away, wondered what Frost had meant by *his* share. There was no carve-up for him in the Crick herd or the remuda.

Then Link Sawle was there. Nobody had seemed to notice him coming — he just appeared through the dry, swirling dust. With his hands cupping the horn of his saddle, he sat his horse straight-backed, alongside the marshal, who barely grinned and nodded.

Then, low mutterings ran through the small crowd. Link's appearance had been so sudden it caught everyone unawares. Not even Neck Shippum had the savvy to voice a threat, let alone do anything.

Rachel's eyes darted around, saw beads of sweat running freely down Marlo Frost's face. She stared at Link who sat his horse, calm and patient.

'Mercy on us,' a woman's voice wheezed, breathless, from close by, and Rachel whirled about.

Heavily armed men crowded their horses around a man who sat a grulla stallion. The man was dressed in . . . wore a brown derby. He had thick corn-coloured hair and his blue eyes were riveted on Link.

'Boy Wales!' the woman exclaimed. 'Seen him a few years ago in Limon. He's one unlicked cub, that one.'

'There's some truth in that,' sounded a voice that Rachel immediately recognized. With a start, she looked to her side, reached out a hand to Bose. For a moment, he looked at her without any familiarity, then he returned his stare to Boy Wales. His mouth was working under the heavy moustaches and he was gripping the stock of his big rifle. He turned back to Rachel.

'What in hell's name you doin' here girl?' he hissed. 'As if we ain't got enough trouble. Get yourself over to the marshal . . . now.' Then he kicked his horse towards Boy Wales.

Rachel was startled and sat unmoved. She saw the riders swing their guns on

Bose, but Boy Wales lifted his hand to allow him close. She saw the man mouth a few, faltering words, shake his head slowly as Bose spoke to him.

Mystified at what was happening, Rachel turned to Link. She heard him telling the marshal that if he was wanted for murder, he'd give himself up . . . face the charges.

'You'll be wantin' my gun, I guess?' he said.

'No. You ain't the one I'm worried about, kid. Anyways, my men'll shoot you down if you try anythin' stupid.' The marshal then motioned to Marlo Frost. 'You the one accusin' this 'un of murder?' he asked, nodding in Link's direction.

'Yeah. I've got enough to hang him *and* Marshfield.'

But the confrontation wasn't how Frost had planned things. He felt as though he was losing the high card from an already poor hand. He hadn't reckoned on Lincoln Sawle turning himself over to the law. A rope slung over the branch of a tree had been his plan.

Then Link cursed with amazement as he saw Rachel spur her horse straight at him. She was shouting, her words slapping at him viciously.

'You're a thief and a liar, Link Sawle. If Marlo's right about you . . . I hope they . . . ' The rest of what she wanted to say remained unspoken, as she lurched in her saddle. She would have reached him if the marshal hadn't swung his horse's flanks into her path, ordered her to clear the street.

In the confusion, Link suddenly realized that Frost had got back an advantage. He felt the danger from Rachel's stirring accusation, cursed again as Frost yelled something to the Rolling Wheel men.

Inexplicably he flicked a glance around him, wondered what had happened to Boy Wales. Then he whirled his horse and dug spurs, headed south along the main street. Bose and a few others rode with him, away from the sudden confusion and one or two wild gunshots.

'We done this before, kid. Ride hard . . . that's the secret,' Bose yelled.

Link drew his Colt as he saw four men approaching, crowding close. He aimed at the nearest, saw Bose waving frantically, heard him bark, 'Don't shoot. They're with us.'

Link had another look, recognized the men as those who'd ridden into town with Boy Wales.

The six riders kicked up a dust-storm that rolled through the main street. As they cleared the end of town, Wales's men reined in, leaving Link and Bose to ride on alone.

But Bose was troubled. He muttered and cursed to himself as they rode.

'You been suckin' on prairie dew again?' Link shouted. 'What're Boy Wales's gang doin'?'

'What're *you* doin' . . . givin' yourself up to the law? There ain't even a warrant out. 'Sayin' goodbye to Rachel', you said. Strange that she should turn on you like that. She must've taken you leavin' town, real bad.'

'Rachel,' Link echoed sullenly. 'Reckon she swallowed that story Frost told her, Bose. I kind o' wish she hadn't. My plan might o' worked then.'

'What goddamn plan?'

'Figured that, if I held my hands out to the marshal, it'd look accommodatin'. Nobody can prove that we killed Gil Crick . . . 'cause we didn't. The marshal won't tolerate no lynchin'. So that'd be the end of it . . . an' legal.'

'Now why didn't I think o' that?' Bose laughed. 'Frost's got framed evidence . . . that's what'll hang us, you idiot,' he yelled exasperatedly. 'The man ain't shoutin' his mouth off with nothin' to back him.'

'Yeah. I thought it was a big 'if'. Shame about Rachel, though. She's sure a pretty little thing. You goin' to tell me about Boy Wales, Bose? Tell me what he was doin' here?'

'I don't know that, Link. I really don't. Maybe he knowed Annie Ruggles. He knowed that Frost was accusin' us of Gil's murder . . . we both know that much. When he saw you was windin' yourself into trouble, he acted pretty smart, didn't he? . . . arranged an escort out o' town. But don't ask me any more, Link, 'cause I don't reckon I'm carryin' the answers. Wait 'til we meet him in Colorado Springs . . . tomorrow night.'

'Colorado Springs?'

'Near. A few miles down river . . . along the Big Sandy. There's some talkin' to be done . . . crates to open . . . maybe some to nail down.'

Bose was looking and talking strange again. Link didn't understand, and it irritated him. He'd suffered it before — the time that Bose had told him of his father's death.

'I don't know what's goin' on, Bose. But I ain't throwin' in with no outlaws,' he said.

'You want to go back to Albuquerque

. . . join Mr Silver an' his Vigilante Committee?' Bose sneered.

'What's up with you? Just because I'm bein' called a murderer. Just because Rachel called me a thief an' a liar don't mean to say I am one, or goin' to act like one,' Link returned hotly.

Bose cursed under his breath, and fished out a bottle of White Mule from what seemed to be an endless supply. He took a long pull, licked his lips and took another.

The men rode on, the anger loud in the oppressive silence of the land. It was the first time they'd got snaggy over something they'd done, or were going to do. And it wasn't about any bad words they'd exchanged. It was about something Bose wasn't saying. He had the odd mood about him again, and it wasn't the fault of bad whiskey. Somehow, the man called Boy Wales was to blame.

It was Link who eventually broke the silence. 'You're goin' to throw in with that outlaw? Is that why we're goin' to Colorado Springs?'

'I just told him we'd meet,' Bose growled.

'Well, you do that, Bose. I got other ideas if you'd thought to ask.'

With that, Link reined his horse around and rode off at a lope, headed west towards the foothills. It was a hot-headed, childish thing to do, but he was being tested, and Rachel's outburst *had* hurt him.

Any other time, Bose would have grinned kindly and followed on, as he'd done when Link rode back into Pueblo. But now he'd got real stuff on his mind, Boy Wales had seen to that. Boy Wales was the youngster Bose had known as Jackson Sawle. Boy Wales was Link Sawle's brother.

10

Run to the Hills

The sullen anger and frustration that settled inside Link drove him on through the night. His mare settled into a long, tireless trot that ate up the miles, put distance between him and Bose Marshfield. By the time his resentment had waned he felt a bit foolish, but it was too late to turn back. Long before midnight, he was riding into unknown territory, though he knew he had to be on land crossed by punchers on the Goodnight-Loving trail.

In the vast land, Link was losing his sense of direction. The sky had turned to deep indigo and there were no stars to travel by. Hunched in the saddle, he'd begun to doze when thunder suddenly rolled out from the sierras.

His horse snorted excitedly as a storm fast approached.

When lightning slashed across the sky, broke the blackness, Link read the hands of his silver stem-winder. It was two o' clock, and he reckoned he'd covered thirty miles since leaving Bose. It was only the last hour of thunderhead darkness that had slowed him, and now as the first rain splattered he knew he'd have to find dry shelter soon. He cursed, grinned, as he realized he still wore his shop-bought homespuns. His old clothes were in a slicker roll behind his saddle. For a moment he thought of Rachel — probably because she'd admired the tailored suit, then he spoke reassuringly to his horse, led it gently forward.

He told himself that come daybreak, he'd head off towards Colorado Springs, meet up with Bose. Then the storm broke with a ferocity that turned him breathless. Hailstones the size of Minié balls pounded his head and shoulders, made his horse whinny and skitter.

They walked the bed of an arroyo until the horse found an overhanging cutback and Link swung to the ground. He pushed himself in hard against the dry wall, crouched in the lee of his mare. He closed his eyes and hung on to the bridle reins, let the storm do its worst.

Lightning ripped the sky apart and thunder numbed Link's ears. He had no idea how long the storm lasted, only that it was a long time, that it had been foolish of him to seek shelter in the arroyo. The torrent of high-coloured water swirled around his thighs and he recoiled from the touch of drowned critters, gnarled sticks that looked like snakes, blowdown from the distant sierra.

He thought of the Rolling Wheel herd that was camped back along the Canadian. The storm was moving south; Link reckoned it would be two hours before it struck. He remembered that in Pueblo, he and Bose had learned that Marlo Frost had called in his cowhands. Except for a few nighthawks, they'd mostly all ridden to Pueblo to rope in Bose and Link. That meant there wouldn't be enough riders to hold a big trail-herd if a lightning storm broke. The cattle could stampede across fifty square miles or more.

'Scattered like a sheepherder's thoughts,' Link sniggered. 'It'll take Frost and his men a week o' Sunday's to make a gather.' He grabbed at the horn of his saddle, shouted for the mare to move. He hung on, kneed its belly until it scrambled around and up the side of the cutback, out of the arroyo.

Then Link remembered that the cattle and horses now belonged to Rachel, and suddenly he wasn't quite so amused or full of himself.

'Her father's been murdered; Frost's already twisted her mind with lies, and her trail herd's probably just about to run itself clear across Colorado,' Link reasoned. Rachel Crick was likely to have as much fun in Pueblo as his own ma did. Link squeezed his eyes shut, shook his head violently at the quirk of fate. He wasn't sure it was the ending he wanted.

'I'll find Bose in Colorado Springs,' he shouted into the storm. 'He'll figure somethin'. That's what he's good at.'

Out along the bank of the arroyo, the land became more broken, and after a half-hour's harrowing ride he stopped beside a gnarled, weather-beaten oak. He slipped from his saddle, pulled at the tie-strings of his slicker roll. With the rain still powering down, he managed to exchange his sodden homespun suit for his work clothes. He pulled on the slicker and hauled himself back on to his unhappy mare, drifted with the storm.

It was nearing first light when the storm eventually let up, when the rain turned to drizzle. He was dry enough, but cold and shivery. His hands were cramped and he rode humped in the saddle as he followed the course of the arroyo.

Near where the land spilled into the vast featureless plain east of the Rockies, he pulled to a halt. In the distance, through the drizzle and darkness that preceded dawn, he'd seen a flickering pin-prick of yellow light. He considered it for a moment, brushed water from the brim of his hat and rode on.

He realized that in following the water-filled arroyo, he'd found a drovers' shack. It was a crude wooden construction that provided minimal shelter for trail hands, a hard-earned sod roof, half-way between Pueblo and Colorado Springs. As well as the dirt box, there was a lean-to in which stood three disconsolate horses, and no smoke rose from the tin-pipe chimney.

Link hitched his own mare to a loop of greasewood and slipped through the darkness towards the cabin. Through a window crack he could see three men. They had a jug which they'd been passing round. He could hear their loud, whiskey-slurred conversation, figured they'd been driven off the trail by the storm. He recognized one of them; a Rolling Wheel cowhand who'd given mouthy encouragement to Marlo Frost, when he'd wanted to hang Link and Bose.

Suddenly there were a lot of things Link wanted to know, and the men looked likely givers. He took a side-step, pushed the flat of his boot against the door. The mouldy planks crashed open and he went in, gripped his Colt beneath his streaming slicker.

The sodden, foul-smelling atmo-sphere rolled into Link. He grimaced, heard sharp intakes of breath as the men turned towards him.

'What the hell!' the Rolling Wheel man uttered. He peered hard at Link. 'Don't I know you ... from some-where?' He then wondered aloud.

'Yeah, I reckon we might've met,' Link said. 'I want to know about Marlo Frost an' Dog Kerlue. You tell me what you know of 'em.'

The man couldn't immediately recall under what circumstances they'd met previously and, after a moment's hesitation, he talked.

'Marlo wants Gilmer Crick's cattle and horses. He's got a mind to marry 'em . . . along with Crick's daughter. But Dog reckons it's easier to run 'em off. Sell 'em and quick an' pay us a fightin' wage. I'd naturally go along with that . . . with Kerlue.'

'Yeah, you would. Keep goin'.'

'Dog persuaded Marlo into takin' some Crick men from the Canadian up to Pueblo. All that's left behind with the herd are the Dog boys.'

'What do they want in Pueblo?' Link asked.

'A rooster by the name o' Bose Marshfield. Him an' a younger one he's ridin' with,' the man answered, but slower and more uncertain. 'Dog and his boys move the cattle out from the bed ground an' drive 'em to Colorado Springs. He knows he's goin' to get a good price from Boy Wales.'

The man saw Link's eyes flash at the

mention of the name and he continued quickly:

'Yeah, Boy Wales. Him an' Dog's real close. Dog ain't fool enough to cut Marlo in on the deal. No sir, Marlo Frost's lost himself a trail herd.' The man ran his tongue along his bottom lip. 'And this is the good bit,' he said. 'Without her cattle, Gil Crick's gal ain't much use to Marlo, if you get my drift.'

'Here's to Dog Kerlue an' Boy Wales,' toasted the cowboy who had the jug.

Link looked on confused and bewildered. 'Boy Wales . . . the cattle buyer,' he said. 'What's he like?'

The man laughed. 'His cattle an' his men are from top drawer. Some say he's a man that don't believe much in God . . . a mean son of a bitch. I don't know much more'n that.'

'Where'd he come from?'

The man shrugged. 'South. Folks say he was brought here by his ma . . . some years ago.'

'Which folk? Who knew her . . . his

ma?' Link was breathing heavy. The face of Boy Wales came back to him, the look they'd shared in the street in Pueblo.

'Jigger Crick could tell you, he knew her. He could also tell you . . . Say, mister, just who the hell are you?' the man suddenly demanded again.

Almost casually, Link brought out his gun, pushed it up and under the man's chin.

'I'm Link Sawle,' he said. 'You've probably heard o' me. Me an' my partner, Bose Mansfield?'

'Jesus,' the man stuttered. 'Link Sawle. I thought I'd seen you before.'

Link nodded. 'What do you know about Elias Sawle . . . my father?' he asked menacingly.

The man thought for a second, the response causing problems in his head. 'They say the reason *he* was killed, was 'cause of your ma. Her an' that brother o' yourn sure caused a heap o' trouble.'

'My brother? What do you know of my brother?'

'The Boy Wales, as he's called. It

weren't much of a secret he was their kid. If you're who you say, then he's your brother. You never knew?'

Link's jaw went slack, his eyes widened. 'No . . . no, I never knew,' he gulped. 'I never even guessed . . . not until . . . ' Link suddenly thought back to Pueblo. He recalled the grulla stallion, corn-coloured hair, blue eyes beneath a brown derby hat. Then he swore, as for the first time he considered the names Sawle and Wales.

'What do you mean, it was because o' my ma that my pa was killed?' he demanded of the man.

'It was some words I once heard Jigger an' your ma exchanging.'

'What was them words, Thur?' one of the men said, grinning crudely.

But there was no response. Link took a quick step forward and lashed out, kicked the whiskey jug from the man's hands. It smashed across the floor, its contents running dark into the hard-packed dirt. The two men on the floor were considering going for their guns, but they saw the look on Link's face, the angry set of something personal, saw Link drive the point of his Colt into the Rolling Wheel man.

Link was filled with uncontainable bitterness. From his childhood, he heard his mother's kindly voice, saw his brother Jackson's smiling face, imagined his father's body out on the Staked Plain.

'Get them words right, 'cause there ain't goin' to be a second time,' he snarled. 'Not for any o' you scum.'

'You ain't goin' to kill us. That'd be murder.'

'I know it. But we're goin' to be the only ones who do.' Link thumbed back the hammer of his Colt. 'There's no one knows I'm here.'

'Wrong,' a voice grated, and Link heard the crash of a gunshot from close behind him. He felt as though he'd been slammed violently by the cabin door, and his knees buckled as he juddered forward. His face hit the dirt and he was tasting whiskey when all sense left him.

The two men in blankets swore loudly, kicked themselves nervously away from the body. The Rolling Wheel man fell against the cabin wall, glared at the stain that grew around Link's head.

It was Dog Kerlue who stood in the doorway holding a long-barrelled forty-four. His eyes were cold and the leer on his rain-wet face mocked the dazed men.

'You goddamn freaks. Get up an' out o' here. Get to your horses.'

The cowboys needed no urging, they were getting their fill of ruthless faces. The way the Rolling Wheel man stepped around Link's body brought a rough laugh from Kerlue.

'Dead men don't bite,' he sneered. 'Damned lucky for you I remembered this doghouse.'

As the men gathered up their meagre traps, Kerlue shook his head. He stepped across the cabin, toe-poked Link's insensible body.

'How'd this kid get here?' he asked.

'Marlo was supposed to gather him in with Marshfield.'

The Rolling Wheel man didn't even think to answer. He hadn't got over looking down the barrel of Link's Colt. The whiskey had suddenly turned sour in his gut, and he was airing his paunch as he climbed into his saddle.

The storm had died to a black drizzle and Dog Kerlue was in a touchy thoughtful mood. Neither he nor the three men who'd sought out the drovers' shack, knew what had happened in Pueblo. He was worried, guessed that Link Sawle's partner probably wasn't far away. He didn't want to go up against the old Indian fighter, best get clear away. They'd ride fast south for the Canadian. That's where they were meant to seize the Rolling Wheel herd and its remuda. But the thunder and lightning of the *wet norther* had taken care of that. As Link had done, Kerlue reckoned that the herd was probably stampeded, scattered like chaff across the state.

11

Close Ties

The bullet from Dog Kerlue's big gun had chiselled into Link's scalp. But he wasn't dead. When his eyes worked open, he was almost blinded by the red, stabbing pains, deafened by the angry buzz-flies inside his skull. He rolled on to his side, groped instinctively for his Colt as he listened to the dull echo of a man's voice.

'Looks like you been in trouble, feller.' A man was standing in the doorway of the cabin. 'Who are you?' he asked directly.

'Who the hell are you?' Link grumbled.

'That spirit'll keep you alive, but I'm the one standin' an' I've got a gun. Now tell me who you are . . . what you're doin' here.'

Link dragged his mind into painful attentiveness, listened to the careful, unhurried, Texas drawl. The man didn't know who Link was. That meant he hadn't been riding with the men who'd taken shelter in the drovers' shack. Link wondered what had happened to them; who it was had shot him. Now, looking through hazy eyes, a man he couldn't make out was asking him his name and he didn't have the wit to think up anything bogus.

'Link Sawle. What's yours?' Link thought he heard a quiet laugh.

'The hell you are. I happen to know Link Sawle's in Pueblo. Him and his partner, Bose Marshfield. They're in jail or dancin' with the devil . . . both of 'em. Now, I've wasted enough time 'cause o' this goddamn storm. Tell me who you are, or I'll finish the job some gunny's only half done.'

'I ain't bein' no one else but Link Sawle, mister . . . whoever you are.' With that, Link closed his eyes despairingly.

The man thought for a few moments, then spoke again. 'Well I never knew him by sight. Link Sawle, that is. I knew *Elias* Sawle. That'll be your pa, I guess. I know Bose too. Come to think of it . . . ' The man suddenly stopped talking.

'If *you* ain't got a name, you a government man . . . an agent or somethin'?' Link asked tentatively.

This time the man did laugh. 'I've been called many things, but never them,' he said, looking detachedly around the cabin. 'I sometimes ride with Boy Wales.' Then the man looked with more interest at Link. 'It's funny,' he said, 'but with that hair o' yourn . . . you could almost pass for him. You ever met him?' he asked.

'Boy Wales? No, I never did . . . seen him though,' Link answered, almost wistful.

'Well that's more'n most. Here's your gun, Link Sawle. Reckon you must o' dropped it.' The man held out the Colt, watched as Link struggled to his feet.

'You can tell me who it was took a chaw out o' your head. Lucky you got a thick 'un.' The man laughed again. 'That's somethin' else in common with Boy Wales.'

Link groaned. 'I don't know *who* it was. I only heard the shot. There was three of 'em in here. One was called Thor . . . Thur? They were from the Rollin' Wheel herd.'

The man took off his Stetson, knocked it against the door frame. 'I was trailin' a polecat named Dog Kerlue. I lost the stink of him in the storm, but he was headed this way. It was him shot you I reckon.'

'Yeah. Well as I said, I weren't in a position to see. I'm obliged to you for my gun, mister. You ain't actin' like no hostile, so I'm goin' outside to look for my horse.'

The man smiled thinly. 'I seen it when I rode in. It's a nice lookin' mount . . . bit lonesome maybe. I'll come with you . . . have a look around.'

Outside of the cabin, Link dipped his

neck-cloth into fresh rainwater at the bottom of a barrel. He pressed it gently against his wound, just beneath the brim of his hat. As they stood in the early-morning light, he took notice of the man alongside him. He saw the order, tight and efficient, the clipped moustache, scrupulous eyes.

'You don't have to name me . . . not just yet,' the man said, noting Link's consideration. 'An' as I'm bein' so amenable, I'll tell you somethin' else. Me an' Dog Kerlue ain't exactly friends, if that's worryin' you. An', before he's much older, I'll be whippin' Marlo Frost. Which reminds me,' he clipped, 'Frost claims you an' Bose killed Gilmer Crick. Ain't that the damnedest thing you ever heard?' he added, as Link began to bridle.

'Frost had me an' Bose tied to our saddle horns about the time Dog Kerlue killed Gil Crick. We'd taken some Rollin' Wheel horses away from Kerlue and two of his men. We sent 'em back to Albuquerque, on foot with one horse between 'em. Next time I seen Kerlue was in Pueblo. I saw him . . . not plain, but it was him all right. Me an' Bose never killed Gil Crick,' Link said angrily.

He remembered Rachel's unwarranted condemnation.

'I ain't accused you of it,' grinned the man. 'Marlo's word ain't exactly his bond.'

'There's some that'll believe him,' Link suggested.

'For instance?'

'Crick's daughter.'

The man gave a small, considerate expression, then started to ease himself from his jacket. Link saw him wince, move awkwardly, realized there was a wind of bandages under the man's dark shirt.

'You can wrap me up again, kid, if you wouldn't mind. You're not the only one to take a beating courtesy of Dog Kerlue. Sawbones did a good job, but it's all come loose.'

As Link tightened and tucked the

bandages, the man carried on talking.

'Yeah, good man, that doc. Told me about a young buck who beat up on the town haircutter and two of his cronies. He reckoned that buck got to ride close on Gil's daughter.' The man winked as Link took a step back. 'No you shouldn't worry yourself, kid,' he said. 'Unless that girl o' Gil's has changed, she ain't likely to be takin' much stock o' Marlo Frost. Anythin' she had to say would o' been in the heat o' the moment. Now, you pull them wraps good an' tight. I got me some hard ridin' to do, an' a dog to track down. What you about to do, kid?'

Link pulled up his collar, looked around him. 'I'm ridin' to Colorado Springs. Goin' to find Bose. He's in the pot with Boy Wales.'

'The hell he is. Old Bose? You certain about that?'

'Yeah. As near as I can find out, Boy Wales is takin' delivery on Gil Crick's cattle an' horses. Dog Kerlue's stealin' then peddlin' on the whole outfit. But I

116

reckon you know somethin' about that . . . whoever you are.'

The man grinned and nodded. 'How about you an' me playin' for that pot?'

'I ain't got nothin' else planned,' Link ceded.

'Good. That herd's goin' to be strewn from Hell to Texas. Down there, the rustlers are thicker'n bees on ripe pear. It's goin' to be a short, hard life, but Boy Wales'll pay top dollar.'

Link closely watched the man's face as he spoke. He was certain that the gut commitment came from a family bond, convinced that the man was Jigger Crick. He also knew that the Rolling Wheel cattle, with Gil Crick's road-iron band, were badly scattered. The wet norther had struck with its full, terrific force. It would have been impossible to hold the herd together.

Link shivered under his slicker. For the umpteenth time, he wished he'd never fished the Punta de Agua, wished he hadn't rode away from Bose, wished a lot of things were different.

117

'Glad to see you ain't gettin' too excited, kid. Got to keep tight in a situation like this,' said his companion as they rode. 'We're goin' to let Dog Kerlue gather what he can. Frost an' the Rollin' Wheel cowboys'll be workin' likewise. They can fight off any other cow-thieves between 'em.'

'What do *we* do?' Link asked half-heartedly.

'Wait 'til they've done the hard work, then step in an' take all them li'l dogies.'

'What happens when Kerlue and Frost meet up?'

The man laughed. 'That's somethin' I'd like to see. There's some folk reckon Frost's runnin' scared o' Dog. But I've seen Frost when he's pushed, an' he's treacherous. If he thinks he can't kill a man fair, he'll shoot him down from cover. But I reckon ol' Bose wised you up to them two birds.'

It was interesting stuff, but Link didn't feel good. He wanted some quiet, some time to think, wished the man would shut up. He nodded, gave a deadpan smile. If this man *was* Jigger Crick, then he had sand, could be just as dangerous as Marlo Frost or Dog Kerlue. The men in the drovers' shack had crudely insinuated that Jigger Crick had been more than friendly with Link's ma, and that *she*'d been responsible for the killing of Elias. But Link couldn't see much of that sort of thing in the man he was riding with.

He was tempted to call the man's hand, accuse him of being Jigger Crick, ask him point blank what he knew of his pa's murder. But Link was learning caution. It was like playing poker with Bose. And he was eaten by curiosity, had other important lines of enquiry.

'I couldn't rightly tell from what that man was sayin' whether Boy Wales was a good or bad man. But he reckoned he was my brother. You know him. What do *you* reckon?'

'Listen young feller,' came the quick reply. 'Out here, you only get to grow in that gap between good and bad. An' don't let any two-bit soothsayer tell you otherwise. If Boy Wales *is* your brother, you could do a lot worse than leanin' in his direction. Which is more than I'd ever have said for your . . . well, most other folk.'

'You mean my pa? Well, I never really knew him. He wasn't around much. But 'cause of all the things that's happened . . . what I've heard, I was goin' to kill that Rollin' Wheel man . . . all three of 'em probably.'

'I'd like to be there when you get to Colorado Springs. What you an' Boy Wales has got to talk about should be *real* interestin'.'

Link knew that if it *was* Jigger Crick talking, then he was also Rachel's uncle.

'The Rollin' Wheel cattle were carryin' Gilmer Crick's road brand. They were *his*, legal,' he said.

'Yep. So I've heard. How'd *you* know?'

'Rachel told me. And now that he's dead, the cattle and horses belong to her.'

'I know that, kid. Hell, what cattle we gather's goin' to be turned over to her. You'll be workin' for Boy Wales, not for Dog Kerlue.'

'Yeah . . . right,' Link said, with a little uncertainty. He remembered Bose saying that if Jigger Crick was in Pueblo he'd get to see Rachel, regardless. 'Rachel's alone in Pueblo,' he added.

'I know that too. But 'alone' is mostly in the mind, kid. Take it from one who knows. Anyways, she's got the marshal to look out for her, an' he's a good man. Him an' Gil were close friends. And don't you go botherin' about her lappin' up Frost's lies.' The man looked hard at Link. 'What happened between you, if it ain't too personal? I'm kinda curious.'

Link shrugged, told him how Rachel had publicly sided with Marlo Frost in the main street. How he and Bose had to make a run for it. How Boy Wales had covered their retreat.

The man shook his head slowly. 'I wonder what nipped at the young 'un.

It sure don't sound like her,' he said thoughtfully.

As the two rode together the man continued to talk. Link got more idea of what Bose had meant about Jigger Crick's nature, but the man's eyes never lost their careful look. It was at Colorado Springs the following night that Link experienced the man's daring and cool ability.

12

The Helping Gun

The flat desert land west of the Rockies lay in a permanent shimmering haze. The wet norther had passed, and now a breathless heat hung over the town of Colorado Springs. Beside the swift-flowing Big Sandy, Link Sawle eased out of the saddle and dropped to his knees. He took off his hat and thrust his head into the water, gasped as its coldness brushed the congealed blood of his head wound. Then he straightened, shook water from his hair as a dog shakes its coat.

Fifteen minutes later, he took to the wagon road. He led his horse across a rickety bridge, grinned at a group of children chasing turkeys through a willow stand.

Colorado Springs was a small town

with a single saloon. It was a town where men could listen to news, spend a few hours in the company of others who lived on excitement and danger.

The man Link was riding with had stopped at a single-storey house at the edge of town to ask questions. Then he followed on, watched the clapboarded, sun-baked buildings for any sign of trouble. Link was waiting for him, half-way along the narrow street.

'Are they here?' he asked.

'No. Bose is with Boy Wales though. The whole outfit's pulled out. Gone to round up the herd.'

'What about Kerlue . . . Frost?'

'No sign o' Kerlue. Frost and some of his men were in town earlier on. I've spoken to someone who reckons Bose ain't too far away.'

'What do you think?' Link asked.

'Ladies that live on the edge o' town don't normally make mistakes about what men are around.'

Link smiled, looked up and down the street.

'Yeah, take note of where we are kid,' the man said. 'The livery opposite has always got fresh mounts. You never know when they're goin' to be needed.'

Link saw the livery, noticed the thrown-back doors, heard the snort of stalled horses.

'We'll take a look around,' the man went on. 'It shouldn't take long. Then we'll go back to see Miss Hattie . . . get us some rib-sticker. Might be, we'll sniff out Bose's lair. The thing is, I don't want anybody to see me, not just yet. But I won't be far away. While you're lookin' out for any of the Dog Kerlue gang, or Rollin' Wheel hands, I'll be lookin' elsewhere. But I'll be close . . . the town ain't that big. Just don't do anythin' foolish.'

A little further down the street, outside the saloon, Link flipped the reins of his mare across the hitching pole. He rested the palm of his hand on the butt of his Colt, knew it was the heat of the day keeping folk out of sight. He heard a sound beside the false-fronted building, took two steps back to check it out. He looked almost directly into the rising sun. He couldn't see the men, didn't know whether there were two or three of them. They were mounted as they came at him, but he was half-blinded by the brightness of the light, couldn't make out any faces.

He thought of the man he knew as Jigger Crick, wondered where he was, as a shout rasped out at him.

'You still aimin' to put a bullet in me, Sawle? Now it's my turn, an' nobody much knows we're here, either.'

Link felt the icy chill run across his shoulders down his spine. He groaned as he recognized the voice of the man called Thur, and because it was too late and he had nowhere to go.

As he moved his hand to his Colt, Link was suddenly grabbed, pulled back against the front of the saloon. He fell to one knee, was pushed aside as the man stepped around him. The man fired a Winchester, immediately levered in another round. Link drew his Colt, but it was no use. The man had already fired again, was hurling abuse at the men who'd appeared so deadly and threateningly from beside the saloon. Before Link could get to his feet he'd fired again. Through a swirl of gun smoke he saw two riderless horses backing their way across the street. Another rider was skewed half out of his saddle. He was barely managing to stay on his horse, clamping a hand over the spurting wound in his shoulder.

It was when Jigger Crick stepped out into the street that Link saw one of the attackers. Thur Chawle had thrown himself from his horse, crawled low to the corner of the saloon. Link brought up his Colt and drew back the hammer. Chawle looked at Link and oozed cold sweat, gripped his gun with both hands.

For a moment Link held his aim, then moved the Colt a fraction before touching the trigger.

'This'll just hurt a bit,' he said grimly, before putting a bullet through the fleshy part of Chawle's upper arm.

Blood spurted thick and red from the wound, immediately soaked Chawle's sleeve, splattered his shirt and pants. Chawle let out a tortured yell, kicked himself back against a low wooden step. Link rose and stepped forward, kicked Chawle's gun under the ground timbers of the saloon. 'Somebody *did* know you were here, scoui-breath.'

The second man had dropped his gun, clung one-handed to the horn of his saddle. The third was lying dead in the street, his upturned face already caked from the dust of his own horse's pounding hoofs.

The man who'd been Link's companion for the past two days was pressing fresh shells into the chamber of his rifle. 'I had to be real quick, kid,' he said. 'I reckoned these were the men you were tellin' me about. Was I right?'

'Not the one who shot me, but they were the others, yeah. The one called Thur. He won't be doin' much gun-work for a while.'

'Hmmm. One got away. But I almost

took his arm off. He's another won't be doin' much brand-burnin' either. Let's get out of here.'

Link turned to look down the street to consider the situation, then he saw Bose as he stepped from a door-way, went down on to one knee, his old Sharps rifle up and ready. As other men came piling out of other doorways and the saloon, Link cursed, then couldn't help but laugh.

At the sound of gunfire, there they were: all the old-timers, looking for the trouble. *That* would have been the most effective way to find Bose, if Link had thought about it. Fire off a few rounds into the street . . . shout a bit . . . wait for him to come running.

Link made a grab for his horse and called out. Bose looked around quizzically, shook his head and made a cautious move forward. He carried his gun at his hip, and Link noticed it was levelled just beyond and to one side of him.

'It's been a long time, Jigger

. . . maybe too long,' Bose said, the pitch of his voice low and intimidating.

'I just goddamn knew it,' Link cursed and stepped between them. He reached for Bose's gun, pushed the barrel down towards the ground. 'No, Bose,' he said calmly. 'You know Jigger's — '

'Meet me at Hattie's, Bose,' Jigger cut in. 'Whatever's between us can be settled there.' With that, he flicked a glance at Link.

Link nodded. 'It was when you spoke about Rachel Crick. That's when I knew who you must be,' he said smartly and turned to Bose. 'Everything's goin' to be just fine,' he added. 'We'll both be there. An' there'll be no gunplay, Bose.'

Without another word, Link and Jigger saddled and rode off. Bose crossed the street to the livery to get his own horse. He exchanged profanities with himself for the full five minutes it took him scowling to the edge of town. When he entered Hattie Darling's house where Link and Jigger Crick

130

waited, he held his gun at his side. His eyes flicked, glittered as he sensed a scrap.

'Put the cannon away, Bose,' Link said.

'You keep out o' this,' Bose snapped back. 'Me an' this son of a blue ticket got a few words to exchange, an' most of it ain't for your ears. Go on, clear out. Wait for me by the bridge.'

'The hell I will,' said Link. 'If it weren't for Jigger, I wouldn't have a tale to tell. You an' me been friends a long while, Bose, so I'm not havin' you get tangled in a gun argument. You could o' told me Boy Wales is my brother. And now I know that — '

'Do you know that it was Jigger Crick killed your pa?' Bose interrupted.

Link spat, blew air through his teeth.

'So that's it,' he said. 'Well, if that's how it pans out you won't mind if it's *me* that squares the deal, will you? . . . seein' as how it was *my* pa.'

'Who told you it was *me* killed Elias?' Jigger asked Bose.

'That's somethin' I've known for a while. Elias knowed you was gunnin' for him. He told me he was goin' to find you to learn why. He never supposed it was anythin' to do with his own missus until it was too late. You knew he was comin' after you . . . even goaded him into buyin' a gun. But he could never stand up to you, Jigger. With him out of the way you were free to dance with Ruth . . . or so you thought. Pity you didn't let her in on your plan. Ruth loved you, Jigger, of that I'm sure. But killin' Elias was the meanest and dumbest thing you ever did . . . an' that's for sure.'

Bose took a deep breath, looked miserably at Link. 'That's the way this man sorts trouble Link. Puts bullets in it.'

Before anyone could say or do more, a man appeared in the open doorway behind Bose. He was wearing an unusual brown derby hat, and he wasn't looking at either Bose or Jigger. His blue eyes were looking directly at Link.

Link stared back at him, the colour draining from his face.

They had no ready words to swiftly draw the years together. Jackson Sawle of Bar Ranch, who'd become Boy Wales of Colorado Springs, had buried his brand in the years since he'd left his family. And time had eroded the softness of youth, the mischievous smile that Link sometimes remembered wasn't there. Their father killed it with his stern brutality, something he'd mistaken for authority and discipline. The brothers didn't speak. They just stood there looking at each other. Link knew then that he reviled his father and what he'd done.

Almost as though he read Link's thoughts, Boy Wales pulled something from his pocket. It was a small stone with a hole through it. Many years ago, he'd laced it into one of his boots, worn it to a Sunday prayer meeting. Link recalled his brother getting a whack for irreverence.

'I heard about you,' Boy Wales said,

quietly. 'They were callin' you 'game-cock' in Albuquerque. You sorted out some funsters . . . didn't use a gun.'

'Yeah. Perhaps we could band up an' share our talents. Just think about it, Jack. You an' me takin' on the cow-thieves.'

Before he'd finished, Boy Wales was ready with an answer. 'You don't know what you're talkin' about, an' you ain't ridin' with me, Link. Go back to Bear Ranch,' he said emphatically. 'Your life's there. You don't want anythin' to do with me. Forget we ever met.' He turned on his heel.

Link was stunned, his mouth opened and closed. He bit his lip, looked around, hurt and uncomfortable. Both Jigger and Bose appeared to be taken aback by the exchange.

'Yeah. He's given you good advice, son,' Bose said uneasily. 'Time we was movin' on.'

'Who'd be without family,' Jigger Crick muttered derisively, as Link and Bose left Miss Hattie's place at the edge of town.

★ ★ ★

Jigger walked his horse back into town. Link and Bose nodded an impassive farewell, cantered their own horses across the bridge. Link had a look towards the stand of willow, but there was no sign of the kids who'd been chasing turkeys.

It was nearly an hour before Bose spoke. 'You can't brood, Link. Listen to what I got to say.'

'I wanted to do that before, Bose, but you never said anything. What's different now?'

'It just is, Link . . . that's all. It just is.' Bose tried an uncomfortable grin, rode close up as they rode south, as he explained.

'I got me an outfit together. A few of the Rollin' Wheel boys that didn't fall for Marlo Frost's lies. Then some more that was spit-disgusted with Dog Kerlue an' his workin's. We got most of the remuda they spilled, a full chuck wagon and a keg o' trade whiskey.'

135

Bose looked eager, slapped his horse's neck. 'Be like ol' times, Link. Me an' the very best firewater. Come on, cheer up. You know what they say 'bout an ill wind.'

Link was thoughtful as he watched Bose laugh at his own little joke.

'That mean norther has spilled cattle all over the landscape. Even the mavericks'll be a rustler's dream. We been spendin' too much time in town, son. Gettin' soft. Mixin'. Listenin' to talk an' the like. What we both need is hard cattle-work, a few nights under the stars. I'll be ramroddin' the best outfit between Mexico and the Canadian line. I'll make you a top hand, Link. With that schoolin' o' yours . . . a top hand bookkeeper. I can guess what's eatin' at you, son, but after a week, you an' me will have such a herd o' longhorns an' Durhams, that you'll need a 'scope to see across 'em. Here, take a drink. Stop you lookin' like a sick calf.'

Link swore incredulously as he watched Bose pull out a bottle of his favoured White Mule.

'Here, meet the family,' Bose said, handing Link the bottle.

Link coughed, choked on the first pull. 'What happened between you and Jigger?' he wheezed.

'We sort of drifted apart. He chose your ma.' Bose chuckled, reached out for his tequila.

13

The Running Brands

When Boy Wales had so brusquely
turned him away, Link was more deeply
hurt than he could remember. But Bose
didn't talk about it. Through the heat,
the dust and the bawling of the cattle,
he pushed Link into his work: long
hours in the saddle that began before
sun-up. No time even to wash the dirt
and sweat from his aching body.
Making the gather, riding herd was
hard and dangerous work. Scarcely a
day passed that one of the men didn't
exchange gunshots with speculative
raiders.

The norther had been one of the
most crushing and violent in years. It
had panicked several trail-herds, drifted
cattle from the range of big and small
outfits. Punchers from all spreads were

138

working with Bose's men.

Early one evening, before first dark, as Bose and his cowhands were approaching the hold-up ground a mile or so from the Canadian camp, a big man with cropped steel-grey hair rode in from the east. He was driving a rig, had four riders in support.

'I know him,' Bose said. 'Tater Jimes. He's the *hefe* in this neck o' the woods. It'd better be me ride out and talk to him. You stay here, kid.'

'Like hell I will!' Link responded sharply. 'We're havin' no more o' that nonsense, Bose. We've treated his cattle right and if he don't know it, it's time somebody told him. *I'll* talk to him. *You* stay behind. You can unwrap the big fifty, though.'

Bose grunted. 'Yeah. Remember what I told you. That man gnaws on wagon wheels.'

Link grinned as he rode out to meet the formidable cowman.

'Who's roddin' this rustler spread?' Jimes bellowed.

'We ain't a rustler outfit, an' you know it,' Link answered back. 'We gathered over two hundred head o' your strays. Everythin' that was wearin' your iron, was turned back on to the range. That ain't rustlin', mister.'

Jimes sniffed, eyed Link carefully. 'What right you got to be workin' this range? What cattle do you or Bose Marshfield own that gives you the right to work for strays? Answer me that, young 'un?'

'Better us than anyone else,' Link said confidently. 'But I already told you what's happened to your cattle. You knew they were grazin' on your own land before you rode out to ask.'

The cowman snorted, rubbed his stubbly chin. 'If you're short o' hands . . . good hands, I can help you out,' he offered in a curious change of approach. He glanced over Link's shoulder, and Link turned in the saddle, saw Bose approaching with a sly grin across his face.

'Bose,' Jimes called out a greeting. 'Is

140

this the youngster they're callin' the gamecock?'

'It is. And I'll wager you've already sized him up right. You knowed his father . . . Elias Sawle.'

'I did too. An' I didn't like him,' Jimes flicked a glance at Link. 'Sorry, kid.' Then he turned back to Bose. 'What's this about you stealin' them wagons at Colorado Springs . . . puttin' your men on Rollin' Wheel horses?'

'The coosie that was drivin' the wagon an' a couple more buckaroos got 'emselves roostered . . . kind o' lost their bearin's. They plumb forgot who they was workin' for, so I gave 'em a job. All heart, that's me. And them ponies belong to Crick's kid . . . Rachel. She can have 'em when she's ready. They're safe enough with us.'

'You sure are a couple o' honest Johns, Bose. But they're still accusin' you an' the youngster o' murderin' Gil.'

'Yeah, I know. You believe that, Tater?'

'If I did, I'd have had you both shot

from the saddle . . . would o' done it myself.' Jimes looked out across the range. 'Send your wagon over to the ranch house. Tell 'em to load you some fresh food.' He smiled large. 'But don't go readin' me wrong, Bose,' he rumbled. 'I ain't about to trust you further than I kick horse apples. It's the gamecock, here. He looks an' sounds more decent and law-abidin' than you ever did. I heard what happened to Shavin' Sam an' his cronies.'

Then Jimes addressed himself to Link. 'A year or so back I dozed off in his chair. I was tired of his prattle. The jackleg trimmed my eyebrows. Taken me nearly fifty years to grow 'em. It might sound kind of odd, but I owe you, kid. I just wish I could o' seen you cuff him.'

Link nodded his acceptance. 'Why'd you not do it . . . there an' then?' he asked.

Jimes laughed. 'Ha. Reckon I'll never know the answer to that, boy. My Achilles heel maybe.' Jimes had another good, snorting laugh. He moved his rig in a small arc, fixed his penetrating eyes back on Bose. He leaned in close, thick gnarled hands holding the reins. 'Just one more thing interested me, Bose. Why you runnin' a Lone T brand on some of the strays?'

'It's an iron we're pushin' into every critter I find that was in that Texas Pool herd. The herd that was run off by Beck's Landing. You remember that?'

'Yeah, I remember, Bose. I asked *why*?'

'It was Link's idea. To divide the takin's among the widows. A share-out for them an' childer left behind by those that were shot dead.'

'Yeah, that figures. *You*'d never come up with anythin' that charitable, eh Bose? You bookin' yourself a blessed restin' place?'

'Gettin' me some insurance. There's nothin' wrong in that.'

Jimes removed his Stetson and fanned his face. 'I'm parched Bose . . . could do with a drink,' he said. 'I'm

143

bettin' you ain't trailin' dry.'

'I never do that, Tater. Let's go.' Bose rammed his rifle back into its scabbard and turned his horse back towards the drive camp.

Good-naturedly, one of Jimes's punchers bounced his horse's flank off Link's mare. He grinned. 'Funny kind o' name, 'Tater',' he said. 'It comes from when he first started out in the cattle business. He was so poor, he lived off potatoes. He took his rest on a bag of 'em . . . made whiskey from 'em. They say he even used to pay wages with 'em for a while.'

The man flipped Link a cut of chaw tobacco. 'You was right about him . . . Jimes, knowin' what your layout was up to. Me an' some o' the boys been watchin' you for a week or more. He's easy on the trigger with rustlers. They been the curse of his life.'

'Yeah. I heard him cursin' Bose for a rustler.'

'Bose Marshfield? Hell, that old range tramp likes to make out he's a big-time brand-artist, but most know better. That's right, ain't it gamecock?'

Link winced at the name coined in Pueblo, but he grinned and nodded. 'I guess,' he said, spitting juice. He watched the two tough old-timers ride slowly to where the chuck wagon rested atop a low-rising mesa.

★   ★   ★

It was well into full dark when Bose and Tater Jimes left camp. Jimes set his horse's head for home, then sprawled shaky in his rig. Bose showed up at the herd unsteady in the saddle. He was working a slick grin across his face.

'Old Tater's taken a shine to you, kid. He's sendin' over a keg o' double rectified. Says it's a thank you for somethin'. Don't reckon him an' my trade whiskey hit it off.'

The following morning, because he wanted a quicker working of the range, Bose split the outfit in two. He was going to take a pack outfit and drift towards the South Platte. Link was to work south of the Arkansas towards the Canadian.

'Take Jimes's men and the Rollin' Wheel cowboys that quit Frost,' Bose said. 'I'm takin' Dog Kerlue's deserters. We'll maybe take us a little *paseor* . . . see bad men along the Purgatoire.'

* * *

The following day Link was joined by three other riders who said they were from the Half Moon ranch. Link recognized them and voiced his unease to his men.

'They could be with the Half Moon now. But when I saw 'em in Pueblo, they were with Dog Kerlue. It would o' been them that bought some o' the Texas cattle from him. Look at this,' he said.

He smoothed the dirt with the sole of his boot, picked up a greasewood stick and drew the Rolling Wheel brand. He looked at it for a moment then changed the configuration. 'See how you can make it into a Half Moon?' he asked the group of punchers.

He gave a thin, deprecating smile. 'You boys know that when Marlo Frost ran Gil Crick's Lazy C iron on the Rollin' Wheel cattle, he did a real gentle piece of work ... too gentle. He hair-branded most of 'em. That's why Bose said to stamp 'em with the Long T, if Crick's iron didn't show. Well, they'd haired over so much, we branded nigh on a hundred head.'

'Crick gave Marlo a hard time over that,' said a Rolling Wheel man. 'Before he pulled out for Albuquerque, he told Marlo to rebrand everythin' that wasn't proper burned. Yeah, when he reached the Canadian, he sure give Marlo hell about it. I heard him. But Marlo never rebranded anythin'. That's where he brought you an' Bose in.'

'Yeah, I remember,' Link said. 'Who owns the Half Moon?' he asked a Jimes man.

'Difficult to know for sure, but Mr Jimes reckons it's Dog Kerlue.'

'Makes sense,' Link groaned, thought exactly the opposite. 'In the mornin' we're ridin' a big, big circle. Gather everythin' in the Half Moon iron you can find . . . and any other brands. We're claimin 'em, goddamnit.'

'That'll call for fightin' Link.'

'Maybe . . . maybe not. But blow the dust from your shooter barrels,' Link said and hauled himself back on to his mare.

The next day Link sat thoughtful in his saddle. He watched a few minutes tick by on his stem-winder, then he placed it carefully back in his suit pocket. From all points, long strings of bawling cattle were being driven to the hold-up ground. He heard a doleful song drifting through rising dust, hoped the singer would make it through to night camp.

Though the day was already hot, he felt a chill run across his shoulders down his spine. All of a sudden the sun seemed less bright, the vast Colorado sky not quite so blue.

He made certain he had a fully loaded cylinder in his Colt, rode down the slope into the dust-haze. Somehow it seemed safer to become part of it. He wasn't afraid, just recalled some words of his father's about killing not being fit work for any man.

14

Round-Up

Link and Abe rode into the herd. Abe was a hard-bitten Running Wheel cowpuncher whose loyalty to Gilmer Crick was a proved one. For more than an hour the two men cut out Rolling Wheel cattle and marked them with Crick's road iron. After they'd looked through the mixed brands, made sure they'd worked the herd clean, they rode to the flanks of the round-up. Three men were containing the steers they'd cut out. The other riders sat their horses and held the main bunch.

'The Half Moon stuff need to be cut,' Link said. 'We'll start with that big calico. Wasn't he the marker . . . the lead steer in Gil Crick's trail herd?'

'Yep, him or his twin brother,' Abe said. 'But the road iron has wore off. It was one o' them clumsy jobs of makin' the Rollin' Wheel into a Half Moon. For Chrissakes, a greener could see that's a worked brand. Anyway, there ain't a man in the outfit hasn't eyeballed that steer at some time.'

A Tater Jimes hand, with one of the Rolling Wheel men, had been sitting between the main herd and the cut, keeping tally. When Link and Abe cut a critter, they'd shout the brand and the tally men would echo it before marking up their books.

As Link and Abe rode past them, Link spoke with a steady confident voice.

'We're startin' on the Half Moon stuff.'

Together, he and Abe rode into the herd. As if by some predetermined signal, the punchers who took their orders from him and Bose manoeuvred themselves so as to be handy if and when trouble started. Unnoticed, they covered the men from the other outfits as well as those from the Half Moon.

Link cut the calico steer past the Half Moon trio and the tally men. He sang out doggedly: 'Rollin' Wheel. Tally him up and rebrand. It's one o' Gil's, and there's more comin'.'

Then he rode to where the three Half Moon punchers were flanked by Rolling Wheel men. He climbed from his horse. He groaned, stretched his back and spat into the hard ground.

'You saw that steer I just cut out, an' you heard what I said. But I'll tell you again, just to make it clear. I'm cuttin' all Half Moon stock into the Rollin' Wheel herd. Before first dark you three are goin' to snatch up every Moon critter and burn it with Gil Crick's Lazy C road iron. Now, anythin' you don't like?' he challenged.

'Them's Moon steers. They belong to the outfit we're workin' for. We ain't sticken' 'em with someone else's travellin' road brand. We're already gettin' the rawest deal, an' we ain't about to take orders from a snot-nosed pup.'

'Get down, mister. Get off your horse,' Link said, brusquely.

As the man swung down from his saddle, Link took a step forward. He waited for the man to turn towards him, then swung the back of his hand hard across the front of the man's face. He waited until blood ran free into the man's thick moustaches. 'It was *Gil Crick* got the rawest deal, you scum-suckin' pig,' he rasped savagely. 'Now, before this snot-nosed pup gets angry . . . who *does* own the Half Moon brand?'

'Leave him be,' one of the others said. 'We've heard about you an' your fists. It's the mark of Dog Kerlue an' Marlo Frost.'

Link swore. 'Yeah. Two vipers in a nest. As if I didn't know.' Slowly Link drew his Colt, turned the barrel into his wrist. 'Now, without fists,' he said. 'Let's see if a pistol whippin' softens that iron resolve.'

'You ain't doin' that to us,' the mounted man warned.

Link shrugged, put his gun away. 'Yeah, you're right,' he said. He looked up at the Rolling Wheel men. 'Noose 'em.'

It took the men little time to expertly slip a running coil over the heads of the Half Moon men. They dallied the tag ends around their saddle horns.

'It's nearly a two-hour ride back to camp. If my boys see any cottonwoods on the way, they might just be tempted to bend a bough,' Link said with a dangerous, sarcastic smile.

Link and Abe rode back into the herd. As they began cutting out Half Moon steers, Link saw punchers from the other small outfits heading for camp. That meant they were taking their string of horses, pulling out for home. Link smiled. He understood they didn't want to take the trail of the Half Moon men.

For the next few hours, the three sullen Half Moon men roped Half Moon steers, sulkily branded them with Gil Crick's Lazy C road iron. They finished soon after dark, but didn't take supper. They quit camp, drove their short string of horses into the dust.

'Old Tater himself couldn't have made a neater job of it,' said a Jimes hand. 'A passle full o' anger, but not a shot fired. That's sorghum lickin' good.'

Link was sensible enough not to crow over his bloodless achievement. He knew the likelihood of trouble before they got back to Pueblo. He doubled the night guards, was taking no chances on a surprise attack or stampede.

'Don't go forgettin' what happened to those Texas men a while back,' he told them, even though he knew they were seasoned hands, all of them giving him a few years. He laughed to himself, knew they'd never make a bad move or let *him* make one.

Late that night around the camp-fire, the men were going through their familiar banter, their jokes, the entertainment of getting life sorted.

'What I can't figure,' said Abe, 'is why Kerlue or them Half Moon cowboys was ever fool enough to work the brand on that big calico steer. We knowed the beast better'n our own womenfolk. It sure cinched our bet on what they'd been doin' to the Rollin' Wheel brand.'

'That's what I reckoned, when I roped and throwed him.' Link grinned. 'It's what I hoped when I run that Half Moon on to his backside.'

'You? You mean . . . that you? Well I'll be hornswoggled . . . '

The branding of the calico steer was another story that Tater Jimes would savour, add to young Link Sawle's burgeoning credentials.

★   ★   ★

For a further seven days and nights they worked hard. They were running low on flour and sugar and the men were spinning out their tobacco. Link wondered how Bose's keg of trade whiskey was faring, his saddle-bag store of White Mule. The men were getting

156

resentful and ornery with less than four hours sleep out of every twenty-four. They growled at one another, and even the horses were ganting down and fractious. Link was invariably the first man to saddle after a poor rest. He drove himself harder than his men and they knew it, it helped to keep the lid on. They all rode leg-weary horses into camp, put away beans, thin gravy and a biscuit, before saddling a fresh horse. To keep up their branding rate they moved camp twice a day.

'A man don't need a bed to work with this outfit,' a Jimes man said.

'*You* don't,' Link agreed. 'We're doublin' the guard again tonight, an' you're takin' bobtail.'

When Link was alone, riding night herd, he felt the burden of anxiety; things he wouldn't share with his men for fear of worsening their already low morale. Bose and his men should have been camped near, but they were a long day overdue. Link hoped they really hadn't met 'bad men' on their detour along the Purgatoire River.

Link eased up on work the next day. It was to give the men and horses a rest, he explained. In fact, he wanted time for Bose and his herd to arrive from the South Platte.

While most of the men rested up, he saddled himself a good horse and cantered from the camp. A Rolling Wheel man watched him as he rode through the spread of grazing cattle.

'None of us should stray too far. Marlo Frost's camped not far west o' here, and he's got a horn drooped. Them Half Moon curs will o' got back by now, and they won't o' forgot the big calico. You best not ride alone, son. Take one of us along, why don't you?'

'I'm ridin' *north* to take a look. I won't be anywhere near their camp, but thanks,' Link replied.

Riding towards Two Buttes Creek, Link wondered what Rachel Crick was doing, what she was thinking, back in Pueblo. Jigger had told him that the marshal would look out for her. But it wouldn't help her with the 'not knowing'. He'd never sent word that he and Bose were working to gather her cattle and the remuda. She'd called him a rustler and believed Frost's lies about the murder of her pa. But Link's comeback would be when he gave the herd back to her. Until then, she could think up as much bad stuff as she wanted. For a few moments Link experienced a warm feeling at his chivalrous sentiments.

He topped a low rise, looked down on a bright ribbon of fast-running water. He looked for Bose, but saw no sign of him or the trail herd. He dismounted and loosed off his saddle cinch, then he sat down in the shade of his horse's belly. Well screened by greasewood from any riders, it was as good a spot as any to keep a look-out. It commanded a good view of the country to the north, across the creek.

He sat there in the rising warm. Within minutes, the utter weariness of his body got the better of him and he dozed, his chin dropping to his chest.

It was almost mid-afternoon when he jerked awake, snorting, making a grab for his Colt. He took a few deep breaths and wound his stem-winder, saw it was two and a quarter hours past noon. And then he caught the sounds that had probably woken him. They were slightly below, off to the right, where the creek forded. Half-way across, he saw a mule team hitched to a low-sprung brake wagon. Its wheels were held in the mud and stones, and a rider was looping a saddle rope to the wagon's splinter bar, shouting orders to the team driver.

Link was bemused, then quickly astonished. The horse-rider was Rachel Crick.

He sat quiet and swore, again thought of Rachel and her wanton public outburst against him. He wondered how much more she knew about him now . . . his family background. He could see what she was doing, but where the hell was she going? he suddenly wanted to know. He was innocent, was doing all he could to help her, and the only place she could be heading off the trail to was Marlo Frost's camp.

He swore again as he pulled himself up, walked the horse gently away from the rise. As soon as he was out of sight of the river, he swung back into the saddle. He headed his horse west, rode hard in the direction of where he estimated Frost to be.

He was still angry after an hour when he spotted the two riders. They were well ahead of him, headed across his path. He drew back, rode a big arc, until he reckoned he would intercept their route. He found a rock-strewn hollow, and in the lee of some tangled chaparral, tethered his horse. He set himself up with his Colt and waited.

15

Return to Colorado Springs

As the two men approached, Link Sawle's voice cut through the over-whelming silence.

'Hold up, Frost. Just stop ridin'. From here I can't promise a good clean shot. I'll probably take off your great ugly head if you make me pull the trigger. The same goes for your Mexican friend.'

The horsemen checked, held their hands away from their guns.

Link shouted again. 'I saw Rachel Crick a ways back. If she's comin' to see you, Frost, she's way off the trail. But I'll take you to see her . . . both o' you. Unbuckle your guns an' do it real careful . . . back your horses off.'

'We do that an' he kill us,' snarled the Mexican.

'If I'd wanted to do that, I'd o' done it by now,' Link answered back. 'Oh no, I want Rachel to know the truth . . . the truth about her pa.' Link moved out of hiding, held the Colt steady in the crook of his arm. 'Head for the trail that leads to the crossin' on Two Buttes Creek. You'll hear me breathin' real close behind you. Break into anythin' above a trot an' I *will* start shootin'. Get goin'.'

Link close-herded them ahead of him. He watched closely, looking for the dupe, the sudden movement, the appearance of a concealed gun.

Marlo Frost also suspected a deception. Contrary to what Link Sawle had said, he didn't believe Rachel Crick was anywhere near that part of the range. He'd last seen her at the hotel in Pueblo where she'd left him in no doubt of her antipathy towards him. She'd told him to bring the herd in. Told him that if he lost any of the remuda or the cattle, he'd be answerable. She'd ensured the marshal was there, and even he'd grimly suggested that Frost take notice of her words.

Frost was carrying a small belly-gun. It was tucked into his waistband behind his pants belt. It was of little use to him at present though. Link was wary, had them both well covered. Frost needed to move and he was nowhere near close enough for the small-calibre bullets to put Link out of action. Meanwhile, he'd ride in sullen submission, bide his time, wait for the close-up chance.

Had Link been less wary of his captives, he'd maybe have sighted the rider who appeared on a distant ridge. The rider came in from the south, sat watching for some minutes before riding off to the east.

Frost was taken aback when, thirty minutes later, he sighted Rachel Crick riding ahead of her mule team. He'd quickly accepted Link's undertaking; to get a declaration of guilt about Gilmer Crick's death. He swore to himself, felt his mouth running dry. To confess to any of it would, at best, be as good as putting his head in a noose. His only chance was to silence Link. He brought to mind the startling revelation of Link's being Boy Wales's brother. As they turned from the ridge, down towards Rachel's wagon, he pitched a question out over his shoulder.

'You and that outlaw brother o' yours been playin' a smart, long game, ain't you, mister gamecock?'

'I didn't know he was my brother until a few days ago. Now shut your mouth, Frost.'

Frost smiled thinly as they rode down to the creek. Now he had another weapon.

As they approached Rachel, she nudged her horse from the water, levelled her pa's scattergun.

'I was wondering how soon it would be before help arrived,' she said without much humour.

'What makes you think it's help? I brought your Romeo back,' Link called out unkindly. 'He's goin' to tell you a few things I reckon you should know before your relationship blooms. An' you can put up your gun, you ain't in any danger.'

Link walked his horse to the driver. He levered a shell into the breech of his Winchester, handed it up. 'Don't know how the hell you got into this, mister, but I hope you know how to use this. It's for the pepper-gut. If he moves, kill him. Don't think on it . . . just pull the trigger.' Link turned partly to Rachel as he spoke. 'If you've a problem with it, he's one o' the vermin helped kill Miss Crick's pa.'

'That was Dog Kerlue,' the Mex blurted. The man was scared, suddenly eager to talk himself out of a nervous bullet. 'Marlo knows I never had anythin' to do with killin' of Gilmer Crick. He tell you. You ask him what — '

'Shut it,' Frost barked. He looked hard at Rachel. 'I brought men to Pueblo to prove that Marshfield and the kid here killed Gil. And they had help ... the *cabron* they call Boy Wales.'

'That's a real bad mouth you got, Frost. Now I just want to beat the truth out o' you. Get down,' Link fumed. He rapidly unbuckled his gunbelt, hung it over his saddle horn and swung to the ground. 'I'm real sorry Rachel. This ain't the kind o' thing you should be watchin'. But I want you to hear what lover-boy's got to say. You can close your eyes if you want, just don't think of ridin' off.'

Frost had the advantage of height and a few pounds. He sneered as he unhurriedly dismounted. Maybe now he wouldn't need to use his belly gun. He smiled up at Rachel, then faced Link.

'Let's see if the gamecock's as good as they say. Not just a scaredy li'l bobwhite.'

Link's anger, his recklessness, rushed him forward. But Frost had primed his young adversary, and was ready for the assault, stood firm. He looped up an

arm, his fist crashing full into Link's
face. He drew back his arm, struck
quickly again as Link staggered off
balance. Link retched, turned and fell,
grasping at Frost's lower legs. Both men
then went down.

Frost was a master of all-in fighting.
But it was new to Link and he was on
the defensive . . . and unsuspecting. He
was taking close punishment from
Frost's fists, didn't go for the biting and
gouging and kneeing in the clinch. The
low blows were hurting, but he was
tough and held on to Frost, kept him
tight until he got a breath.

He managed to break away, and
scrambled to his feet. Frost was fighting
dirty. His teeth had taken a hunk of
flesh from Link's arm and a corner of
one eye had been raked with a broken
fingernail. But Link kept his head,
didn't rush in again.

Drained of colour, Rachel gripped
the horn of her saddle with one hand.
With her other, she held the scattergun
so tight her knuckles glowed. The blood

and the brutal thud of body punching, the rising smell of men's fearfulness made her stomach heave. She thought that Link was getting the worst of the beating, didn't know that he looked worse than he felt.

The two men circled warily, then they slugged and swung, missed and connected. They took it in turns to smash in a punch, ward off a blow with a shoulder or forearm. They fell, then rose from the ground, confrontational in ghoulish palls of alkali dust.

But Link was gaining. He had the advantage in years, had better wind and got the advantage of it. Frost was getting tired and Link was learning to avoid his frustrated rushes, kept him on the move. Frost's breathing was long and rasping and his legs were failing.

Link was now standing back, taking measured swings at the man's face, neck and upper body.

'For Chrissakes, ease up,' he panted. 'All you got to do is tell Rachel the truth. You don't have to die out here.'

But the blood was roaring loud in Frost's ears. He took no notice, continued with his pushing forward, the senseless wild swinging of his fists. Link was gaining control. Several more times he knocked Frost down, waited restlessly for him to rise. He thought of kicking the man's head to finish the fight, but then thought of Rachel and held off instead.

Frost was staggering from side to side with lung-bursting sobs. Like Link, his face was smeared with blood and slime from the roughing he'd taken. Link took a step forward, sent Frost down one more time with a poled fist to the side of his head. He swore, closed his eyes at the immediate pain that spread through his hand.

Frost had landed heavily on his back. He blinked into the sun, rolled on to one shoulder, then his stomach. He pushed his left arm against the dirt and tucked his right one under him, blew exhausted air through his teeth.

'Reckon you got me beat, kid,' he

growled. 'Them fists done a heap o' damage.'

'Then tell me . . . tell Rachel, who killed her pa. I'll start usin' my boots next, an' that ain't nice. Who killed Gil Crick? Tell us.'

Frost was kneeling. 'Yeah, sure,' he groaned. 'Perhaps 'gamecock's' about right.' He spat some thin blood, pressed the knuckle of a thumb tentatively against his mouth. Then his arm swept outwards and up from under his body.

Link stared as the short-barrelled belly-gun roared up at him. He twisted towards Rachel as if for support.

'He had another gun. The scum . . . ' The words stopped as he stumbled one pace forward, groped space. As he fell sideways, a second bullet ripped into the flesh of his neck.

Holding out his gun, Frost staggered to his feet. He looked up as Rachel screamed, as she reared her horse, jumped it straight into him. One hoof pistoned into his shoulder, another struck him in the middle of his chest.

He crumpled without a sound, lay in a motionless heap.

Rachel leapt to the ground, and ran towards Link who was breathing deep, clutching his stomach. Blood was pooling in the scoop at the base of his throat and his face was twisted with pain. His other hand was outstretched, clawing at a clump of cheat grass and he was saying 'stupid' over and over.

'Has he killed you?' Rachel asked with curious detachment.

'No. He should o' got closer . . . just hurts like hell. But thanks for your help . . . sorry about the mess.'

Rachel flinched, looked at her blood-stained hands. 'You're welcome,' she said with the trace of a smile sounding in her voice.

Link held out his hand and Rachel helped him to his feet. He swore and puffed air, looked beyond her towards the horizon and a small group of approaching riders. They were shimmering figures in the rising heat-haze, but they were unmistakably coming from the east, the general direction of where Link reckoned Frost's camp to be.

'They must o' heard the noise we been makin',' he said tiredly.

He looked hard at the brake-wagon, decided there was no time to unload the trunks and boxes. He stepped up to the frightened driver. 'Keep that gun pointed at the Mex. Just get down quick,' he told him. Then he snapped at the team reins and yelled. Already fearful, the mules baulked and swung around. Immediately, the wagon tipped over, with a grinding wrench of wood and metal joints.

Link put his hand into the transom and drew the linkage pin. 'Dumb brutes ain't gettin' far pullin' all this stuff,' he muttered. 'Tie the reins to the seat irons,' he told the driver. 'They're just about set to run to the border . . . give Frost's men somethin' to run after. You take the Mex's horse and mount up. Ride north . . . we'll follow.'

'What about these two?' Rachel asked.

'What about 'em? They ain't dead . . . yet, which is about as lucky as you can get.' Link glanced hostilely at the Mexican. 'An' Frost needs a nurse,' he threatened.

★ ★ ★

When they arrived, two of Frost's men attended to their ramrod's wounds and two of them took off after the front section of the brake wagon. Two more rode half-heartedly after Link and Rachel.

After a few miles of hard riding Link sighted his own men.

'We've outrun the hostiles, Rachel. Straight ahead . . . those are *my* punchers.'

But Link's improving mood was just as soon dashed when he saw one of the riders was a Bose man. He had a darkly-stained dressing around one arm and his face was haggard with fatigue and pain. The other men wore the look of those who were part of bad news.

'Dog Kerlue's men. They jumped us,' said the wounded man. 'Two . . . no, three nights ago. They stampeded the herd . . . shot us up.'

'Where's Bose?' Link's voice was a dry, harsh whisper. 'What happened to Bose?'

'He's all right. It's Boy Wales. Kerlue shot him at Colorado Springs. He said he wants to see you . . . sent me lookin' for you. It don't look like the sort o' wound that heals.'

Link swallowed hard, let the name of Dog Kerlue sink in.

'Yeah, OK, but I can't go visitin' lookin' like this,' he said with grim, biting wit. He didn't see Rachel watching him, didn't see the lack of warmth in her eyes.

'You come back to camp with the rest o' the boys,' he told her. But he was distracted. 'I've got somewhere to go . . . somethin' to do.'

Rachel knew of Boy Wales as the

leader of an outlaw gang. She'd only seen him once in Pueblo, at the burial of Annie Ruggles. She recalled the blue eyes beneath the funny brown hat, the lovely grulla stallion. She'd seen him talking to Bose Marshfield. It was when she'd accused Link of being a thief and a liar. She'd heard the man called Boy Wales tell Bose to get Link away from the town. The outlaw had said he'd provide riders to cover them. He'd said to take Link to Colorado Springs. Rachel had remembered . . . always thought it strange.

She broke from her thoughts, realized Link had moved his horse up close.

'I've got to go. He's my . . . ' he was saying.

'Yes, I know,' Rachel answered.

'You know?'

'Yes . . . I think so. Just go, Link Sawle. We'll make out.'

They exchanged an intriguing, private glance. Link wanted to make a stinging remark about losing his whole family. But instead he turned to Bose's man.

'Let's go,' he said.

Without a look back, the two men set off towards camp, then Colorado Springs and the Big Sandy.

16

Hard Travelling

Link was surprised to find the marshal of Pueblo sipping coffee at the camp.

'I thought you were lookin' out for Rachel,' he said.

'I was. But I had to go out o' town on business. I weren't gone more'n a day. I didn't expect her to up sticks an' leave. Where the hell did she think she was goin'?'

'I'm not sure. Perhaps she wanted to get involved. She's the sort. Anyways, she'll be here directly. You'll be takin' her back to Pueblo?'

'That's what I'm here for. I'll cuff her if I have to.' Town marshals have their own way of news-gathering, and the marshal of Pueblo already knew most of what there was to know. He knew about Boy Wales, about Link Sawle, where he was going. 'Contrary to what most folk think, there ain't a lot wrong with Boy Wales,' he said to Link's astonishment. 'You see, what they don't know is that most o' the time he only stole cattle from cattle-thieves. Kind o' poetic in a way.'

'Yeah, it's almost admirable, ain't it, Marshal? I'm told he's holed up in Colorado Springs.'

The marshal nodded. 'It's where Jigger Crick took him after he'd been shot.'

'It was Dog Kerlue?'

'Yeah. Seems like Marlo Frost had seen Jigger in Pueblo. It was the day of Annie Ruggles's funeral . . . the same day you came in. Frost told Kerlue that Jigger was alive. Kerlue caught on that your bro . . . Boy Wales, had set a trap for him. So the dog that he is, he trailed him back to the Big Sandy. That's where he shot him. It's always been the best defence. Now you and Bose got to keep yourselves alive.' The marshal looked hard at Link. 'Looks like someone else already started on you.'

Link smiled grimly. 'They're just flesh wounds, Marshal. I got no busted bones. I'll get 'em cleaned up a bit . . . staunch the bloody flow.'

'You do that, kid. I'll take care of Rachel. We'll hold the herd till Tater Jimes an' his men get here. Rachel asked me to sell her pa's cattle. Jimes bought 'em with the remuda. Paid a good price too. An' in case you're wonderin', he's also sent men to help Bose.' The marshal looked wryly at Link. 'You sure done yourself a good deed outside o' that haircutter's. Old Tater Jimes thinks you've got the very sun tucked up behind you.'

It was with doubtful emotions that Link saddled a fresh horse and headed for Colorado Springs. He saw it as a race against the death of his brother and he set out at a fast canter. But there were no relay horses, and he knew he'd need to gauge his pace. It was also dangerous country — where there'd been reports of Comanchero activity

180

— and the marshal had wanted to send a man with him. Link would have none of it though, reckoned one man would be less noticeable, less valuable than two.

As he rode the cut-up country east of the Cristos, Link thought through his life. Not for the first time did he wonder how all the trouble had happened; what his part was in it; what was left.

It was mid morning, and he was picking his way cautiously along the dry bed of Fountain Creek. He heard the restless shuffle of another horse and reined in, listened. He drew his Colt and turned to look behind him, heard the nerve-jangling voice.

'Ehhhhhh gringo, you lose your way?'

Link whirled his horse. But behind him, along either side of the banks, were lines of advancing riders. Within moments they were around him, crowding and hassling. His horse eared and lunged as men reached for and pulled on the bridle reins. Hands grabbed him from the side, pulled him from the saddle. Link fell, swinging his arms, trying to club someone with the barrel of his Colt. And then something hit him hard on the side of his head and he was out cold before he hit the ground.

Fifteen minutes later he woke to blurred sounds and images. He was lying on his side, his ankles were roped together and his arms were pulled tight behind his back. In the grey early light he looked up at the coarse leering features of a big man, with long greased plaits. He had a skinning knife in his hand, was testing its blade with a gnarled thumb. Then he grinned, spoke through gapped and broken yellow teeth.

'We start with the ears,' he said thickly.

Link caught the odour, winced at the man's fetid breath. He remembered Bose saying that with Comancheros, *you smell 'em long before you see 'em.*

There was no doubting the intentions

of the man. Link had heard that one about the ears. Though his head was splitting with pain, his predicament enabled him to think very clearly. He was in the hands of a group of *mestizos*: human jackals who'd usually show isolated ranchers, trail herds, even wagon trains, no mercy. They were constantly on the move, known and feared for their wanton cruelty.

'Do your worst . . . see if I care. I ain't got no money, an' the horse ain't mine,' Link blustered. 'So take out the last of the Sawles. There's no one much to miss *me*.'

'Ha. Which ear then? Or maybe a choice finger?'

'I'd heard about your bloodthirstiness . . . lots of other things,' Link hissed. 'But not your stupidity.'

'You call me stupid? What you mean, brave little man?'

'How much am I worth without ears? Nothin' much. Without fingers? Even less.' Link mocked. 'But *whole* . . . in Pueblo? I'd say much

183

whiskey . . . much gold if you knew who to see . . . *brave big man.*'

The man turned his head slightly to one side, spat a stream of dark juice into the dirt, close to Link's face.

'You say, you got some resale value? But what you say, that worth, if I hang from a tree, eh? Big belly shot full with holes . . . good whiskey runnin' out? For me, that not much fun.'

Link sighed, squeezed his eyes shut.

'OK, do your worst. Of course, me not turnin' up in Colorado Springs is goin' to make *some* men *real* angry.'

'Pah, what men?'

'Boy Wales's men. It'll be them come lookin' for me,' Link ventured.

'Why?'

'Because Boy Wales is my brother.'

The big Comanchero was suitably, visibly, shocked. He moved back a little.

'He don't have no brother . . . no family.'

'None that you know about. But have a close look at me. You see the resemblance?'

The man thought long. 'Maybe. But maybe . . . you . . . trick . . . me?' he said, thoughtful and slow.

'I'll leave mules to do that. My name's Sawle. Wales is just a mix up of the same letters. It's what *he* did. Many years ago he felt the same way . . . mixed up.'

One of the other men stepped forward, looked down at Link. 'I think perhaps I seen this one before. I seen him with the old one, outside Pueblo. Why don't we take him in? Get the reward maybe. You cut off *everythin'* if he's lying.'

The big man's eyes rolled, then he growled with laughter. 'I like that, *amigo*. Free his hands and legs. We eat, then we ride . . . find out if he's worth gold.'

One of the gang who was less drunk than most of the others offered Link a dry tortilla and some cold beans, whiskey to dull the pain. Link guessed the man who'd hit him was suddenly worried about confronting Boy Wales.

The miles and hours went by and it was nearly full dark when they eventually saw the lights of Colorado Springs. Link was told to ride ahead to the house at the edge of town. It was where he'd last seen his brother. Hattie Darling answered to his call, and Jigger Crick appeared behind her. The lady couldn't see how Link was set when she beckoned him into the candle-lit room.

'I'm roped to the horse,' he told her.

The renegade who'd given Link some food rode up. He cut the cinch hobble from Link's ankles, watched charily as Link swung stiffly from the saddle.

'The doc's been,' Jigger said as Link stepped on to the low veranda. 'Said the odds weren't good. I wonder what he'd give you?' he added.

'I keep tellin' people . . . these're nothin' more'n flesh wounds, an' I'll be all right. Where is my brother?'

'Room at the back. He's taken in a big measure o' laudanum. You want some? Might ease them *flesh wounds.*'

Link held up his hand. 'I told these men there'd be payment for gettin' me here. Tell 'em why, could you?'

Jigger turned to face the Comancheros, reluctantly called out. 'He's Boy Wales's kid brother. If you want payin', I suggest you come back. Right now ain't a good time,' he threatened.

The Comancheros muttered amongst themselves, discussed dire repercussions. Then, with menacing gestures, they swung their horses away from town.

Link pushed open the door to see his brother, smelled the raw mix of blood and sweat, blinked at the heavy opium tincture. He saw the oily gleam across Jackson Sawle's grey face as he hunkered beside the cot.

'Well, I got here. Had a bit o' trouble on the way . . . but nothin' I couldn't handle. How about you?'

'Yeah, I had the same. Didn't come through as well though. It's good to see you, Link. You goin' to tell me about you . . . all the stuff I don't know? Better not make a meal of it,' Jack grinned, coughed at his morbidness. 'Go on, tell me,' he grated. 'I ain't goin' to die unless I know how you got to look like walkin' wolf meat.'

'Ha. You should see the other feller.' Link placed his hand shyly on his brother's forehead. 'You don't go quittin' on me Jack. You already done it once. Don't do it again.'

'Reckon it's too late for family feelin', Link. But I still got to tell you about me.'

'There's nothin' I really want to know. Maybe somethin' about Ma.'

Jack moved his body slightly, shivered from the pain.

'You tell that Rachel Crick I weren't such a bad man, eh?' Jack's eyes closed. 'Tell Jigger I want to see him,' he said, his emotion spent.

Hattie Darling was unnecessarily lighting more candles. She muttered something inaudible, looked tired and used up, as Link passed through the house. Jigger was outside, staring into the silent darkness.

'Go see him, Jigger,' Link said. 'Try an' stop him from dyin'.'

Link sat down on a bench, felt very alone. Again he drifted off into the past, tormented by the dreams of his ma and pa and Jackson. He didn't hear the footfall on the veranda, hardly registered what Jigger told him.

'Sorry Link. There's some things you just can't stop a man from doin'. Your brother just died.'

17

The Gather

'We ain't made to carry that much lead in us, son,' Jigger said as, with their backs to the sunrise, they rode from Jackson's grave.

Link looked at the horse he was leading — the grulla stallion that Jigger told him was now his.

'Dog Kerlue should never have done that,' he said with quiet intensity. 'Now I got to find him . . . tell him.'

For a long moment before speaking, Jigger considered the inevitability of Link's threat.

'Whatever Jack was goin' to tell you, Link, it would o' been clouded with all sorts o' regret . . . hurt maybe. If you want, I can tell you somethin'. Only if you want, that is. Bose must've told you about me an' your ma?'

'Yeah, some. He reckoned you killed my pa. Tell me about that. Did you kill him, Jigger?'

'No Link, I didn't. I ain't sayin' I didn't want to, 'cause, I did . . . real bad.'

'Why? What happened?'

'Hmmm. It's difficult to know exactly where to start.'

'How about from when she left . . . took Jack to Pueblo? You know about that?'

'Yeah. It's where I first met her. She was pretty desperate, an' that ain't good for a nice-lookin' lady in a town like Pueblo . . . not with a yonker an' all. I reckon she was close to doin' herself in. No friends, no one to turn to. Anyways I found her some work an' some lodgin's. She soon got well, but she wouldn't leave me . . . got real attached. She felt she owed me, I guess. But we never got further than that . . . except for our feelin's, if that's what you were thinkin'.'

'I find it hard to think anythin' at the

moment,' Link said. 'You just carry on talkin'.'

'She told me about your pa. That made me real angry . . . him forcing her to that state. That's when I realized I wanted to do somethin' about it. But she said she'd leave me if I did. Well I'd kind o' got used to her by this time. She said that if there was punishment to mete out, she'd be doin' it.'

'She took Jack. Why'd she leave me behind? Did she tell you that?'

'No, she never said. Sorry.'

For the next fifteen minutes, neither man spoke. They followed the course of the creek towards their camp. But it was obvious that Jigger had more on his mind, more that Link wanted to know.

'The bastard stood in the way of what I wanted,' Jigger said. 'And what your ma wanted, if she'd o' but said. Your pa had to go. I'm real sorry Link, but that's the way it was.'

'So you did shoot him?'

'No. I told you. I wanted him . . . warned him a couple o' times. I

192

told him to get himself a gun, be ready to use it when we met up.'

'What about Bose? They were close friends.'

'I know. I told him I'd take 'em both on, if I had to. I figured Bose had some sort o' hand in the way Ruth got treated. But I was wrong about that.'

'Yeah,' Link agreed. 'I'm sure lookin' forward to makin' camp. Get me some rest from all o' this.'

'Well, there ain't a lot more to tell,' Jigger said. 'Elias showed up . . . met the drive one night as I knew he would. I asked him if he'd got himself a gun, but he hadn't. There was no need to let anyone else know. What we had in mind was private, between me an' him. I never really wanted to shoot him. It was close, but no one had yet met their Maker. We talked, agreed to settle it with our fists. I did anyway. I told him to wait for me where I'd be ridin' herd later that night.'

Link was listening to Jigger as he pointed. It was still four or five miles distant, but he'd seen the rising dust of the herd.

'Biscuit n' coffee in an hour,' he said half-heartedly.

'Yeah, just about time to finish my story,' Jigger countered. 'Where'd I got to?'

'My pa was waitin' for you to kick the stuffin' out of him.'

Jigger smiled tolerantly. 'It was some time after bobtail watch. I was goin' to quit the herd . . . ride out to meet up with Elias.' Jigger laughed. 'I don't know whether he'd thought about it, but I'd given him the opportunity to bushwhack me if he'd lied about not carryin' a gun. Anyways, after I'd rode in circles for a spell, I got to thinkin' he'd scuttled. Hah. That's where *I* got shot. I managed to loose off a couple o' rounds, but got caught again. That's about all I remember.'

'Pa? It was Pa, you reckon?'

'Don't seem likely. It took a couple o' good shots, an' Elias was no sharp-shooter. When I came to . . . when I got some sense back, I was in Colorado Springs.'

'Colorado Springs? Where . . . '

'Yeah, Link. Where your brother died last night. Ruth was there. It was her turn to look after me. When I was strong enough, she said she'd found me when she'd rode out to look for both of us, would you believe. At first she thought I was dead. I was shot up so bad.'

Link looked himself over. 'Yeah, we all know how misleadin' that can be,' he said.

'Elias was dead . . . lyin' not more'n twenty feet from me,' Jigger went on. 'She loaded me on my horse, somehow got me back along the Big Sandy. I reckon it would o' been easier if she'd dug a grave with her bare hands.' Jigger saw the incredulous look on Link's face. 'You can't blame her for not buryin' him. Right then, he didn't mean a spit to her. It was *me* she was worried about.'

'How'd you prove you didn't kill my pa?'

'I didn't . . . couldn't. But she must've known . . . deep down.'

'Why'd you never marry her?' Link asked as a sideswipe.

'Because o' that. There'd always be the doubt.'

'What happened to her . . . my ma?' Link asked after taking in Jigger's reasoning. 'I know about everyone else.'

'She done it again . . . lit out . . . headed north. Men just weren't her thing, Link.'

'No. Not like kids were,' Link retorted. 'What you goin' to do now?'

'Find Dog Kerlue and kill him. That'll do for the meantime.'

Link swore. 'Did you tell Bose any of what you just told me?' he asked.

'No. He ain't ever given me a chance . . . be no point. He knows I was with the Texas Pool herd when Elias was killed. I made a good show near your pa's body too. When Ruth found me she took off my coat . . . left it there. That's what Bose found. Unlike most, he was close to your pa, Link.'

'That's what Bose wouldn't tell me. But then he didn't tell me anythin' much. He knew what I'd do. He guessed you'd have to kill me defendin' yourself.'

Jigger shook his head ruefully. 'Did Bose give you somethin' Link? Somethin' that belonged to your ma?'

'He gave me a li'l rimrock filly . . . a stem-winder when I was growed some.'

'No, after your pa died.'

'No. Nothin'.'

'Old Bose sure kept a few things from you Link. Your ma left her weddin' ring beside Elias's body. It's one a them things a woman'll do I guess. Bose would o' seen it . . . known that she'd been there.'

Link groaned. 'When we were in Pueblo, Bose told me he had suspicions. But he weren't goin' to tell me what they were.'

'Yeah, that was about the time we were settin' the trap for Kerlue an' Frost. Waitin' for 'em to make a deal with Gil's cattle. They figured me dead then. It was later that Frost saw me in town.'

Link took off his hat, wiped his forehead. He was exhausted, still trying to put it all together.

'Bose thought a heap o' Ma,' he said gently. 'He wouldn't have taken to thinkin' she'd had a part in Pa's killin'. He didn't want me to think bad of her.' Link made a small smile. 'He's loyal, if not much else.'

'Yeah, I know. He didn't want to believe any one thing bad about Ruth. But there *was* her weddin' ring. An' it was *her* told Bose where to find Elias's body.'

'I didn't know that.'

'Yeah. She told him in town . . . waited until he was well roostered. She didn't want him chasin' after her . . . or me. She knew he'd try an' kill me.'

'So how does it all stand now?'

'Bose reckons it's up to him to square Elias's debt.'

Link gulped. His jaw dropped. 'You

tryin' to tell me . . . ? That's the real reason you're comin' back to camp?'

'Sure. He wouldn't've tried it before. But now would be the right time, he's thinkin'.'

Link put his hat back on, tugged the brim down over his eyes.

'No you ain't doin' this. It's all about my family remember. That means I have a say. There'll be no more stupid senseless killin'. We'll talk . . . come to some understandin'. Anyways what's the point of a gunfight? You didn't kill Pa.'

'You believe that?'

'Yeah. An' I'm cuttin' you some slack for savin' my life.'

'Christ, there *is* a first time for everythin' all right.' Jigger compassed the horizon as he spoke. 'Even my own brother thought I'd done it. But then, like Bose, he also figured I was in with Kerlue on the Texas cattle deal. It was Frost an' Kerlue led Gil into the trap at Albuquerque. Frost faked a note, signed it with my name. He's as good

199

with a pen as he is with a runnin' iron.'

'What you goin' to do about him
. . . Frost?' Link asked hesitantly.

'He'll be harder to kill than Kerlue.
He's kinfolk.'

'Yeah, Bose did tell me that. 'Shirt-
tail cousin' he said. Did it ever occur to
you that it might be Kerlue that killed
Pa?'

'Yeah, it has Link, many a time. I
guess that really would be your job
then, wouldn't it? Look son, you ain't a
killer. Good with your fists I hear, but
Kerlue's different . . . knows how it's
done.'

'He's been shootin' his way through
my family. I'm goin' to stop him.'

Jigger wasn't going to challenge or
question the set of Link's face.

18

The Price to Pay

West of the Mississippi and Missouri rivers, it was stopping a bullet that settled or ended most disputes. But wealth, and the power that came with it, still carried the most potent force. Along most of Butte Creek's flow, it was Tater Jimes that kept Jigger Crick and Bose Marshfield apart.

It was nearly first dark, and Link and Jigger were approaching the round-up. Tater Jimes had taken his rig out to intercept them.

'It's good to see you back, Link,' he said affably, while admiring the grulla. Then he turned to Jigger. 'This is my range, Jigger. Stretches many times further than you can see in every direction. There's a job to be done, an' I need all hands to do it. So if you've come to lock horns with anybody, forget it. Get another time an' another place,' he rasped.

Jigger held up his hand in appeal, but before he could say anything, Jimes stopped him.

'Right this moment, I don't give a damn about two boneheads bin' on the prod,' he said sternly. 'All I know is, you're working for me . . . all o' you. Now listen good. Dog Kerlue's somewhere out there, an' he's drivin' the tallow off the cattle I bought from Rachel Crick. Well I'm aimin' to get 'em back, then I'm goin' to stretch the hides o' them rustlers once an' for all. That's why I'm payin' you fat money to go get 'em.'

Jimes turned to see why Jigger and Link exchanged a nervy glance, backed his rig horse a few steps as Bose rode up. His voice was a warning. 'Take out whoever you want, but it's Kerlue an' Frost I want.'

'That ain't goin' to be easy,' Bose said, standing off a few paces.

'But it'll explain the 'fat money' you just mentioned,' Jigger added.

'Five thousand dollars apiece.' Jimes made it clear. He turned quickly to Bose. 'That's why you an' Jigger are goin' to bury the hatchet till they're gathered in. You understand?'

'Yeah. Right now, I need the money more than his hide,' Bose replied offhandedly. 'But only until we sweep up Kerlue and Frost. I want to get me an' Link cleared with the sheriff an' Rachel Crick. You know . . . cleared o' murderin' Gil.'

'Yep. I know, an' I couldn't argue with it. How about you, Jigger?'

Jigger nodded, barely raised a smile. 'I got reason to want Kerlue an' Frost planted,' he said, then looked straight at Bose. 'The kid's tryin' to shut it out, so I'll tell you. His brother died last night.' Jigger reined his horse around in a tight circle, rode it to the rope corral for unsaddling.

Bose's face clouded over. He swore massively to himself, looked mortified at Link. He shook his head miserably. 'I'm sorry,' he muttered. 'Link, I didn't . . . '

Tater Jimes flicked his rig forward. He reached out, touched Link's leg with his riding-whip. 'I know he weren't all bad Link, an' he was your brother. For that you have my commiseration.'

Link turned the grulla and his leg-weary horse into the remuda. Then he and Bose walked off a way.

'Did you have a chance to talk to Jack?' Bose asked considerately.

'Yeah, but we never got to say much. He said it was too late. You know . . . for family an' all. I didn't know he meant he was goin' to die.'

Bose was quietly thinking when Link spoke again.

'I know about the weddin' ring you found,' he said. 'It weren't Jigger that killed Pa.'

'Ah, Jigger's got to you has he? Well you heard what I just told Tater,' Bose answered him duly.

Link knew the tone of voice. Knew it

too well to pursue the question of Jigger Crick's innocence. He couldn't think of anything to say to change things. Link knew that his ma had gone north half-believing that the man she'd loved had shot her husband. He took another line.

'He was *my* father, Bose. Do you reckon it's for me to decide about Jigger?'

'It don't make any difference,' Bose answered him gruffly. And then he coughed, changed the subject. 'Let me see that shoulder o' yours . . . get you somethin' to drink, eh Link? You're as peaky-lookin' as a wind-bellied calf.' As the two men walked towards the chuck wagon, Bose threw a chuckler into what he was sayin'. 'Yeah, see if old Tater's got some o' his double-rectified left. You know Link, he showed up here with some yarn about you an' Rachel kickin' the crap out o' Marlo Frost. Hah, I'd sure liked to have seen that, son.' Bose had another short laugh, then turned more serious. 'There's somethin' you don't know about young Rachel. Seems like she got to thinkin' about you an' Jack.'

'Rachel?' Link echoed. 'She's back in Pueblo . . . went with the sheriff.'

'She may be there by now. But she never went straight off.'

'I don't understand. Where'd she go?'

'Colorado Springs. She made a bit of a fuss, so the sheriff went with her. She went to see if there was anythin' she could do . . . for your brother.'

Link stood mulling over the implication, wondered if there was one.

'That ain't a bad thing,' Bose told him. 'Now, let's you an' me find that drink.'

★　★　★

There was no kind of threat that would drag the truth from Dog Kerlue about Elias Sawle's death — how he'd shot him. Bose knew that Elias had been shot in the back. Ruth too, if she'd looked close enough. And Link knew

206

because Bose had told him. Bose had his unshakable way of thinking. He believed that Elias had refused to fight Jigger Crick — attempted to get away after thinking it through. He believed that Jigger shot the fleeing man in the back — an instinctive reaction because of the way he felt about Ruth. And that's the story Bose had conjured up for Link.

'If Jigger Crick got shot, it was *after* he killed Elias. Kerlue, or some o' the other scum. Dixon Dodds or Talbot Hackel. Someone who was with the Texas Pool herd when Jigger wouldn't join 'em. *That*'s where Jigger got the bullet-holes that Ruth patched up. I know what I saw out there, Link. You can swallow the lie that Jigger tells, but not me.'

But Link knew the killer wasn't Jigger Crick. Ruth knew it too. Dog Kerlue knew that she knew, and that would always remain a motive for killing *her*. Link wondered if that was why she'd never returned, stayed up Denver way.

He guessed, almost hoped that Kerlue was the sort of man to taunt him about what he'd done to his family. Kerlue had the cruel streak, would have made a good Comanchero, Bose had said.

'Take one to catch one,' Jimes reminded them when he came to get himself some coffee. 'Bose. You an' Jigger take what men you need.'

'I'm goin' with 'em,' Link cut in, steely and resolute.

'To keep 'em from lockin' them horns, eh? Then again, maybe you've a mind to go it alone,' Jimes said testingly. 'Well, either way I'm gettin' too old to do much about it. I'll stay here . . . look after everyone's interests.'

'I was reckonin' on me an' Link. But if Jigger wants to tag along . . . I'm OK with that,' Bose said.

'Yeah, I can guess why. But it'll take more than three o' you,' Jimes shouted. 'Kerlue will likely have a small army with him.'

'Me an' Jigger know about Kerlue. We both rode with him. You said yourself . . . 'takes one to catch one'.'

The three men left camp, headed north. They rode for a long while, awestruck and silenced by the mighty roof of stars. When they got to where Two Buttes Creek ran into the Arkansas, Bose called to Jigger.

'Do you figure Kerlue'll head for Pueblo or on to Colorado Springs?'

'Colorado Springs. He don't want to mix it with all Pueblo's law,' Jigger answered back.

There was nothing more from Bose. Link knew he was keeping the ill will going, didn't want to open a line of civil communication with the man he'd decided to kill. Jigger knew it and spoke to Link.

'Yeah, ain't just Pueblo he'll be avoidin' neither. Kerlue knows his days are numbered. He can't hide himself in this state — not now Jimes has taken chips in the game. Kerlue ain't goin' to live long buckin' the TJ outfit. Most of his pack will already have tucked their

tails under, hauled freight for Texas
. . . Mexico even. Colorado Springs'll
be wide open, now that — '

Bose broke Jigger's untimely gaffe
with, 'I reckon, that shirt-tail relative o'
yours is now goin' to run with Kerlue.'

Jigger snorted. 'Well, we all got a
cross to bear, Bose. Mine don't come
out of a bottle. An' just remember
before you start chuckin' lead, Tater
Jimes didn't offer many dollars for *my*
hide.'

'They'll have three . . . maybe four
men ridin' with 'em,' Bose said, by way
of a response.

'I know two that won't be with 'em,'
Jigger said after a moment. 'The two
that was with Kerlue when he shot
down the Texas Pool cowboys. I heard
you an' Link met up with 'em in
Albuquerque.'

'There was another reason for
wantin' them dead,' Bose snapped
back. 'But if Kerlue *is* reckonin' on
takin' over Colorado Springs, the
pack'll be back to strength.'

'My guess,' Jigger said, 'is that Kerlue will have toughs with him. Like them leather-slappers that shot you up last week. An' Marlo Frost — that no-good cousin o' mine — he'll stay 'cause he's got nowhere else to go.'

'Maybe,' Bose acknowledged reluctantly. 'Let's get there an' find out. The sheriff an' Rachel are ahead of us, an' we've a-ways to ride.' With that he kicked his horse into a canter.

*   *   *

Long before dawn, a full bright moon lit the surface of the Big Sandy river. The six men riding into Colorado Springs could almost read the stones that marked the graves of the town's Boot Hill. Dog Kerlue reined in. From under the flat brim of his hat, his bleak eyes squinted at a fresh, as yet unmarked grave. Then he rode slowly on.

At the outskirts of town, in the middle of the road, someone had nailed

211

a notice to an upturned water-butt. This time Kerlue reined in. The crude, heavy-handed lettering was plainly visible.

WELCOME DOG —
TO YOU AND YOUR FRIENDS.
WELCOME TO BOOT HILL

'You never mentioned this part o' the deal, Dog,' the man called Boone said. 'I guess we're about to run into the welcome committee who wrote this. Well, my pappy learned me how to take a hint an' I'm takin' the trail to Limon.'

Kerlue made a guttural sound in his throat, pulled the trigger of his forty-four. 'Then you'll take the *long* trail, you gutless dunghill,' he snarled as his bullet caught the man in the middle of his back.

Boone's head snapped back loosely, and as his horse jumped, his body crumpled, toppled sideways. Dust puffed, pale and sluggish, as his body hit the ground. The riderless horse trotted on, its head held sidelong to keep from stepping on the dragging reins.

Kerlue glared at Frost and the other three. 'My pappy taught *me* that the quickest way to cure spine trouble was to take it out.' His eyes challenged, darted from one man to the next. Dixon Dodds grinned faintly and shrugged. Talbot Hackel struck a match to light a half-burned cigarette. The half-breed spat a stream of tobacco juice at the sign.

Frost, whose thin face appeared impassive, was the only one who spoke. 'You sure got a way with you, Dog,' he sniped.

'Yeah. Vamoose. Leave Boone where he is,' Kerlue ordered. He now rode behind, wasn't giving any of his men a free shot at his own back.

Frost dropped back and had a cautious, sidelong glance at Kerlue, felt a sort of dread. He knew he should have killed the man there and then, but of a sudden lacked the nerve. That was the fear that made him sick at the stomach. Sweat beaded on his forehead, soaked the palms of his hands.

So it was, that well before first light, the five men rode into Colorado Springs. They made their way towards the yellow lamps of the saloon, each of them resting a hand on the butt of an actioned sidearm.

19

The Run of Blood

Bose, Link and Jigger Crick took the wagon road into Colorado Springs. So they didn't see the graves of Boot Hill, or the body of Boone that lay crumpled lifeless in the hard-packed dust.

They crossed the rickety bridge beside the stand of willow, rode up to Hattie Darling's house. There was a single candle burning and Hattie waited for Bose's knock before she opened the door. Slumped with distress, she stepped on to the narrow veranda. It was a few moments before she gathered herself to explain.

'I couldn't sleep . . . went to visit 'Boy's' grave. But they were there . . . riding through.'

'Who? Who was there, Hatty?' Bose asked as gently as he could.

'I stopped . . . hid behind the oak . . . saw what he did. It was the one they call the Dog.'

'Yeah, Dog Kerlue. What's he done now, Hattie?'

'He shot one of his men . . . real close . . . just pulled his gun and shot him.'

'Where are they now? They came into town?'

'Yes. They went to the One Tune. I waited, then came here . . . didn't go back . . . to the grave.'

'How many of 'em?' Link asked.

'Five. It was less than an hour ago.'

'There was a peace officer . . . a marshal from Pueblo and a girl,' said Jigger. 'You seen 'em?

'They were here. They left yesterday. I think they went to the grave,' Hattie told them, her voice breaking with wretchedness.

'OK. Now I want to get me justice,' said Jigger, swinging his horse away. 'Let's go burn some powder.'

The three men walked their horses

away from Hattie Darling's house, into the open towards the main street.

Bose eased his .45 in its holster. 'Hattie said there's five of 'em. I'll take three,' he decided.

Jigger was staring into the darkness towards the One Tune saloon. 'Hmm,' he returned. 'That's about what *I* had in mind.'

'Yeah, I was goin' for three, too,' Link claimed.

'An' that makes *nine*. So we ain't gettin' it all our own way,' Bose sniggered.

When the first of the town's buildings surrounded them, they nudged their horses to a trot, rode three abreast. The one main street was less than a hundred yards long and within moments they were outside the saloon. They reined in, looked hard into the deserted town and cautiously dismounted. Waiting with four other saddled horses, Bose recognized Kerlue's buckskin mare. They were stand-hitched, and without fuss Link and Jigger slipped their headstalls, set them free to trot the street.

The three men stepped noiselessly on to the boardwalk, moved to one side of the saloon's batwing doors. They stood listening until the nervous sounding murmur inside went silent.

'Jeez, listen. It's him . . . Kerlue,' Link whispered.

They could hear Kerlue's chilling voice. He was holding audience with a small band of cornered townsfolk.

'We ain't got all night,' he snarled at them. 'I got me a forty-four type writ to serve on you notice-makers. I been real hurt by what I read out there. So you're goin' to take up a collection . . . improve my fortune. You, mister tinhorn in the fancy coat. Maybe one o' you good ladies, an' the thief that's runnin' this crib. You pay up now. An' remember, that Boy Wales ain't ridin' in to save your scabby hides. I've hung his saddle up, real high.'

Outside the saloon, Bose looked from Jigger to Link.

'Just for a while there, I got to

wonderin' why we were goin' in,' he said with a quick shake of his head. 'But not any more.'

'That's my brother he's talkin' about . . . that he shot dead,' Link was quick to respond.

'Get close . . . take a good look. You don't need a reason to kill him,' Jigger pointed out calmly.

Bose stared at the rough wooden planking between his feet, gripped his Colt .45 in both hands. 'Frost will more'n likely shoot himself when we go through the door,' he said.

Link took a deep breath. He thought on what Bose was saying, asked, 'How we goin' to play this out?'

Jigger winked. 'I been thinkin' o' that,' he said. 'I guess it's one big wolf-pack in there. I'm for puttin' bullets into everythin' as we go in. What say you gents?'

'I'm for Link goin' round the back . . . you an' me pushin' in here,' Bose suggested firmly.

His consideration for young Link

wasn't lost. With a nod of his head, Jigger indicated that Link move off around the side of the saloon.

Bose and Jigger watched each other while they waited for Link to get around to the back door

Bose looked sheepish. 'Maybe I got it wrong about you an' Ruth . . . you an' Elias,' he said. 'I never really thought it out much before. An' young Link ain't a bad judge o' character.'

Jigger shrugged. 'That's always been your trouble, Bose. Why'd you mention it now?' he asked.

'Cause this ain't the sort of hoedown you can guarantee goin' home from, that's why. I want to rest easy . . . if anythin' should happen.'

'Then for the sake o' the kid, don't let it. From now on, all you got to do is worry about them in there.' Jigger nodded at the saloon. For a moment they listened, heard the continuing bite of Kerlue's offensiveness.

'Hey, *Margarita*. You must o' known Boy Wales . . . probably had a hand in the writin' o' that note. Tell us about him. I hear tell he spent most of his time crawlin' across dead meat.'

'Hey, Dog,' Marlo Frost shouted. 'Leave her be. The girl ain't done nothin'. Boone could o' been right about this place.'

For two, three seconds, there was an ominous, deadly silence before Kerlue spat his response.

'Another goddamn squawkin' yellow goose.'

A lurid scream merged with the gunshot, and the back door flew open. Link crashed into the saloon making an impulsive and immediate confusion. He didn't have time to look around, to make out Dog Kerlue before the bullet struck him in his chest. He gasped at the massive blow, stumbled backwards and went down. For a second the only sound was his Colt spinning across the floor.

That was when Bose and Jigger yelled notice of their reckless attack, went through the door together. Jigger was to the right, and he was already shooting at Dog Kerlue. Kerlue's face twisted into an instant mask of hate. He stood face on, fired indiscriminately as the reckoning closed in around him.

Bose swung his Colt in an arc, dropped Dixon Dodds who was caught undecided, left it too late. He took Bose's .45 bullet in the middle of his chest. He spun against the bar, looked in vain at the terrified gambler. 'You wouldn't o' bet on this happenin',' he hissed as his eyes rolled. 'I might . . . an' would've won,' were his final words.

His gun blazing, the 'breed shouted something violent at Kerlue. He was shooting at Jigger as he started for the back door alongside the bar. Jigger flinched at the gunfire.

'Take your time,' Jigger called out to him. 'You won't live to tell the tale by bein' hasty.' Then he calmed and steadily took aim, put two bullets low into the 'breed's stomach. 'See what I mean, Geromino?' he said with disgust.

Talbot Hackel had grabbed one of the saloon girls, tight, used her as a shield as he too backed towards the rear door. Wary of his escape, he looked down and behind him for a fraction of a second. From the floor, Link slowly twisted his head up, recognized him as one of the Half Moon branders he'd run out of camp. He made an outstretched grab at his Colt, but the muscles along his arm and in his fingers were numb. Helplessly, he saw the sudden anger in Hackel's face as the man remembered what had happened at Butte Creek. Hackel grinned frighteningly and pushed the girl away, turned his gun down at Link's face.

'Sawle. The snot-nosed pup, that put a rope around my neck. I said I'd kill you for that you . . .'

And then from somewhere on Link's right, and to the side, there came the unmistakable roar of a shotgun. Still only capable of watching the nightmare, Link saw Hackel's face explode in a hideous mask of mangled flesh and bone. The gun dropped from his hand and he fell on to Link. Link came round and yelled with revulsion, managed to kick out with his legs, as some feeling returned to his body.

'You're welcome, kid,' Marlo Frost said, anticipating Link's gratitude as he stepped out from behind the bar. The shotgun fell from his hands as he walked slow and careful towards the batwings. Then he faltered and nodded down at Link, groaned eerily. 'Goddamn that Kerlue,' he managed to say, 'I ain't goin' to make it. The mean son of a bitch killed me.' The dying man managed to push himself through the batwings, make a despairing lunge for his horse. His face turned, caught the first golden streaks of dawn as he fell dead in the street.

Jigger had stood to one side, was pressing his back against the wall just inside the door.

'Anyone else comin' through?' he mused sharply. He pulled back the hammer of his Colt for a final shot at

Kerlue, then changed his mind. He took a few steps across the saloon, and with the toe of his boot he pushed the Colt towards Link's still outstretched fingers. 'You're owed this, Link. Finish the killer off. Put a bullet in him while he's still warm.'

Leaning heavily against the bar, Kerlue was drooling pink from his open mouth. He hadn't got long, but had the doggedness to pull the trigger one more time. 'Three of a kind,' he muttered, almost inaudibly as he dragged up his big forty-four. But his eyes took on the glaze of death, as Link finally managed to squeeze the trigger of his own Colt.

'I got him, Jack. We got 'em all. All those that . . . ' Link gave up his tortuous thoughts. Then his grip loosened and his chin dropped back to the floor as he saw Kerlue's knees give way. Seconds away from death. Kerlue spat froth and bile down the front of his faded slicker.

'I'll see you all in Hell,' he managed before he fell. He twisted his arm, and his gun hand twitched. But his last bullet found its way low into the saloon-gambler's leg.

Bose moved a few paces, stood looking down at Kerlue. 'No one should be able to claim your death for 'emselves,' he said. Then he drew back the hammer of his .45, thudded one, then two bullets down into the dead man's back. 'For me an' Elias,' he said through a trembling jaw.

Link didn't, but Bose saw, then heard Jigger. The unnerving cough was the giveaway; the result of the bullets that had destroyed his chest. Blood was quickly darkening his shirt. He half turned, his eyes searching those few still left in the saloon. Then he looked straight at Link. There was a quizzical smile on his face and an eye twitched as his legs folded, took him gently to the floor.

'Bose was right, as usual,' he said through clenched teeth. 'We didn't get it all our own way.' He was sitting cross-legged and very still — dead by the time Bose got to him.

Bose elbowed aside the few customers who now pressed forward. He looked frantically from Jigger to Link.

'The kid ain't dead. Get him on to a table. Lift him careful,' he seethed at the shocked and horrified faces. He cursed, furiously swept cards and money off a table with the edge of his hand. 'Put him here. Someone get a doctor, or the killin' ain't over.'

The gambling man hobbled a step back. He shook his head, held out his hands as if he didn't want to help. Bose swore at him, smacked him hard across the front of his face.

'Do it now!' he yelled.

On the table, Link blinked, opened his eyes and looked straight up at his old friend.

'Shush, I ain't dyin', Bose,' he said. 'Me parts are movin'. What the hell's happ . . . '

Before he said any more, a man pushed his way through to the table.

'I'm the sawbones,' he blustered

nervously, 'let me see.'

The doctor quickly pulled back Link's jacket, looked at the front of his filthy shirt.

'There should be arterial blood . . . I saw him hit. I don't understand. I'll need something to clean . . . ' he started to say and reached out his hand. One of the girls gave him a damp bar-towel, apologized uncomfortably.

The doctor dabbed and wiped around where he thought Link's wound to be. He frowned, muttered astonishment. From the breast pocket of Link's shirt he removed a battered bit of silverware that was attached to a short chain.

'I think you'll find there's a big piece of lead among these workings.' He grinned. 'It's what saved your life.' He held it up for all to see. 'He looks like he's been kicked by a mule, but he'll be OK. That's more than you can say for the timepiece.'

'The stem-winder. I gave him that . . . must be five years ago,' Bose said, stunned. 'What a gift.'

'A proper lifesaver,' the doctor agreed and handed Bose the battered watch.

Bose ran a shaking hand across his worn-out features, looked hard at Link.

'I never in all my days seen such a mess, Link. Not on anyone still livin' that is. We thought you were dead, lyin' there so quiet.'

Link gave a tired, laboured smile.

'No. I was takin' time . . . doin' some thinkin'.'

'You an' that school-learnin' again. I always knew it weren't any good. What was you thinkin' then, Mister Game-cock?'

'The choices we had . . . earlier on. You know . . . about comin' in here. There's still a lot of unanswered questions, Bose. Like, why the hell Frost an' Kerlue came back here?'

Bose got to his feet, and closed his eyes for a moment.

'Yeah,' he drawled, 'I can see why you'd wonder on that. But everyone's got to be somewhere, Link, an' *here* was their hell. An' as for the unanswered questions . . . there's only one you got to answer.'

'What's that, Bose?'

'Was I right, or was I right?' Bose smiled, then looked disgustedly at the state of Link's clothing.

'If you still got them homespuns, son, you're really goin' to need 'em,' he added more seriously. 'Somethin' to wear on the journey home.'

20

Reckoning

In New Mexico, 'twixt Santa Rose and Tucumcari, the small spread once owned by Elias and Ruth Sawle is now called Bear Horse Ranch. It's worked by Link and Rachel Sawle, and from an upstairs corner room of the house, Bose Marshfield keeps a watchful eye on the day-to-day running. In the corral, the grulla stallion raises its great grey head, snorts its intent at the mares in the home pasture.

During the year's hottest months, Link still drops a catfish line into a deep, muddied pool of the Punta de Agua. At the end of the long summer, a team of wranglers go north. They drive upwards of two hundred saddle-broke horses to the army post of Fort Collins. Once out of Tucumcari, the herd moves east towards the Pecos. But if Link goes with them, they avoid the old Goodnight-Loving cattle trail.

East of the Sangre de Cristo mountains, there's raw unforgiving land that holds more than a thin sprinkling of unmarked graves. They're the last resting places of forgotten men, overgrown by grasses in summer, blanketed by snow in winter. Midway between Albuquerque and the Canadian River though, there's an engraved stone that simply states: GILMER CRICK — TEXAS TRAIL BOSS.

There's some frontier towns that have their own boot hills or cemeteries with more fanciful reminders. But out on the Staked Plain, only a bleak mound of stones marks the spot of the Texas Pool murders. And to the north, five miles from Beck's Landing, there's nothing left of the blackened remains of the tailgate that Link put there to mark the death of his pa.

Along Big Sandy River, near the town of Colorado Springs, a small piece of ground lies tended. No one much notices the lady from Denver who once in a while comes to visit Hattie Darling. Always before she leaves, and alone in the cemetery, she looks sadly at a small marker that says; JIGGER CRICK. Then she places some flowers around another that's cut with the words: JACKSON SAWLE.

THE END

We do hope that you have enjoyed reading this large print book.

Did you know that all of our titles are available for purchase?

We publish a wide range of high quality large print books including:
Romances, Mysteries, Classics
General Fiction
Non Fiction and Westerns

Special interest titles available in large print are:
The Little Oxford Dictionary
Music Book, Song Book
Hymn Book, Service Book

Also available from us courtesy of Oxford University Press:
Young Readers' Dictionary
(large print edition)
Young Readers' Thesaurus
(large print edition)

For further information or a free brochure, please contact us at:
Ulverscroft Large Print Books Ltd.,
The Green, Bradgate Road, Anstey,
Leicester, LE7 7FU, England.
Tel: (00 44) **0116 236 4325**
Fax: (00 44) **0116 234 0205**